The Lady of Solitude

Paula Parisot
The Lady of Solitude
STORIES

Translated by Elizabeth Lowe and
Clifford E. Landers

DALKEY ARCHIVE PRESS

Originally published in Portuguese as *A dama da solidão* by Companhia das Letras in 2007.
First Dalkey Archive edition, 2016

Library of Congress Cataloging-in-Publication Data
Names: Parisot, Paula, author. | Lowe, Elizabeth, 1947- translator. |
    Landers, Clifford E., translator.
Title: The lady of solitude : stories / Paula Parisot ; translated by
    Elizabeth Lowe and Clifford E. Landers.
Description: Victoria, TX : Dalkey Archive Press, 2016.
Identifiers: LCCN 2016031189 | ISBN 9781628971453 (pbk. : alk. paper)
Subjects: LCSH: Parisot, Paula--Translations into English. | GSAFD: Erotic
    fiction.
Classification: LCC PQ9316.A757 A2 2016 | DDC 869.3/5--dc23
LC record available at https://lccn.loc.gov/2016031189

Partially funded by a grant by the Illinois Arts Council, a state agency.

www.dalkeyarchive.com
Victoria, TX / McLean, IL / Dublin

Dalkey Archive Press publications are, in part, made possible through the support of the University of Houston-Victoria and its programs in creative writing, publishing, and translation.

Printed on permanent/durable acid-free paper

Contents

The Umbrella

She opened the letter:

Giselle, I have to tell you exactly how everything happened. Please understand, I absolutely don't want to hurt you. I didn't seek out that woman. I didn't need or want to get involved with anyone else. I met her by accident.

It was raining. A woman was walking beside me. You know, Giselle, how I am, I immediately offered her shelter under my umbrella. I told her I was going to the bar at the corner to have some coffee, as I did every afternoon. She replied that it was an incredible coincidence, because she was heading there for the same reason.

She insisted on paying for the coffee to thank me for my kindness. I refused, saying it was an outdated feminist gesture. She laughed. My name is Charlotte. And mine is Werther, I answered, shaking her hand.

I noticed a flash in her dark eyes. She laughed and said,

But I'm not going to make you suffer like in the book. What time are you coming here for coffee tomorrow? At four, and my name is José. We left the bar together and she told me she didn't have an umbrella and had even stopped buying them because she would always lose them the same day. She also said she had become accustomed to getting rained on and even enjoyed it. I'm just the opposite, I replied, I hate getting wet and, without bragging, I can say I have more than thirty umbrellas from everywhere, English, Italian, French, even those Chinese ones they sell on street corners when it's raining. We said good-bye, she got into a taxi and left.

I went back to the office, and I confess that for some reason she had become indelible in my mind, perhaps her eyes, or her lips, or the sound of her voice. I anxiously awaited the next day to meet her again. That's how it all began, Giselle. To think that I only read Goethe's book at your insistence.

The next day I arrived fifteen minutes early. She was on time. While we drank coffee, she asked me, Don't you think we ought to go someplace where we could be more comfortable? Where, what place? I answered. A motel, for example, she said with total candor. I confess that her frankness and simplicity surprised and enchanted me. I've always hated hypocritical, duplicitous people, and there in front of me was this beautiful woman who was the exact opposite of that. I forgot about the patients waiting for me at the office and didn't even call my secretary. Me of all people, Giselle, who was always extremely meticulous about commitments.

We took a cab and went to the nearest motel. I was more tense than Charlotte was and don't remember exactly what happened on our first encounter. I know we made love. She left before me, kissed me, and said she'd meet me at the bar the next day. I lay stretched out in the bed, remembering her naked body in the mirror on the ceiling.

Again I arrived fifteen minutes early and Charlotte was on time. Over coffee she said, You know, the second time is always better. I called my secretary and asked her to cancel my afternoon appointments.

The second time really *was* better. Charlotte asked for the number of my cell phone. She didn't want to give me hers, and I didn't insist. We set up another coffee date. I asked my secretary to cancel appointments with my afternoon patients, explaining that I'd only work during the morning. Don't ask me why I did it. I don't know.

Charlotte was very discreet in relation to her private life. I knew nothing about her, but she knew everything about me. She never asked me anything, but I told her I was a doctor, general practitioner, married, I spoke about you, about our daughter Maria, the university where I took my degree, the soccer team I root for. She knew everything about me and I knew nothing about her. Not even where she was born, where she lived, her last name, nothing.

At each meeting she became more intense and I responded in the same fashion. My soul overflowed with euphoria when I felt her presence, and I would enter into harmony with the world. At such moments I would stop being me, a forty-year-old man, bourgeois, a family man, and become the other person I always wanted to be, a free man. Only at her side could I achieve that state of happiness. If I knew how to bare my soul, dear Giselle, maybe you'd be able to understand me. Do you remember the day I threw all the umbrellas in the trash, saying that I wanted to be rained on? That was the beginning of my transformation, when I became another man. I no longer had any control over my actions. And don't think, Giselle, that it was easy to admit to myself that I could do nothing to overcome the external forces that were taking control of me. Our stable and tranquil life, which I had always thought ideal, revealed itself to be a great deception. I fled the boredom by working, leaving the house earlier and earlier and returning later and later, and I not only escaped the tedium but also made more money to fulfill my role as provider. I was wasting my life. But we can't live deceiving ourselves, a moment comes when reality proves to be unbearable. Giselle, forgive me for saying this, but I detested, without realizing it, your perfection, your sensible words. I hated our home. I couldn't stand our bourgeois friends, with their country houses, new automobiles, and their wives on diets, working out at fitness centers and bleaching their hair. Maybe that's why I stopped making love to you.

Whenever I kissed Charlotte I would become excited, even if we had made love just minutes before. When I achieved orgasm, I would suffer a kind of loss of my senses, which would last I don't know how long, with scintillations flashing in my field of vision. I liked doing everything with her. Before oral sex, I would contemplate her pubis covered with hair. Charlotte didn't shave, and that thick dark cluster created a dazzling contrast with her snowy skin. She was shut tight, like a safe, which I began to open with my tongue, and from her came a pleasant aroma that excited me even more. I stuck my tongue in deeper and eagerly sipped a liquid that was pure nectar to me. Then she would come in my mouth, screaming with pleasure. Afterward, I would penetrate her with my penis and her vagina was so tight that my member would be chafed after we had copulated for a few hours. On other occasions we would practice anal intercourse, very carefully, and after some time I managed to get my penis all the way inside her. Later I would lick her anus and feel surprise that such a minuscule fissure could be penetrated and still remain unscathed. I would bite Charlotte, but my real wish was to rip off a piece of her flesh and eat it. When we were exhausted from so much

love, lying prostrate in bed, I would put my middle finger
in Charlotte's vagina, then take it out, put it in my mouth
and suck it. Then Charlotte would kiss me and we'd start
everything all over again.

Nevertheless, it wasn't just sex. We would listen to
music—classical, popular, opera, jazz, read poetry to each
other, and prose too. I read to her in bed the *Werther* that
you gave me. I cried, because she was my Charlotte.

My absolute need to unveil the mystery that surrounded
her made me hire a private detective to spy on her. I don't
know whether or not she realized she was being watched.
What's for certain is that she constantly threw the detective
off the scent. He told me that Charlotte would get into a taxi
and he would take another one to follow her, then suddenly
on a two-way street she would jump out of the taxi and
grab another one going in the opposite direction. The detective would lose sight of her. She would enter buildings with
rear doors and by the time the detective realized what was
happening, it was too late. He never saw her with another
person; he kept his camera at the ready, to no avail. He
swore that Charlotte knew she was being watched, despite
his alternating in the task with a colleague. That couldn't be
a coincidence.

Unsatisfied with the detective's information, I decided to
secretly follow her myself, after one of our encounters. The

very first day, Charlotte caught me. She turned a corner, I went after her, furtively, hugging the wall of a building, when I found myself face to face with her, and she asked brusquely, Are you following me, you fool? I was embarrassed at having been discovered and also at being called a fool.

Giselle, you must find it strange that in a letter of this importance I refer to such an irrelevant incident, but it was from that moment that I began to fear losing her forever. Charlotte took two weeks to call me. I couldn't sleep or eat anymore, and I started drinking. Do you remember? I stopped going to the office all that time, I had gastric problems and got a stomach ulcer. I kept the cell phone in my hand for fear of not hearing it ring. She only called me from a blocked number, which kept me from calling her back. Finally, Charlotte called and we set up a meeting for the following week.

Then I made the decision I thought was best. I sold that apartment we had rented out, claiming that I wanted to invest the money in high-return stocks, and asked you to sign the sales deed too. I took the money, went to a jewelry store and bought a diamond ring. As soon as I saw Charlotte, I knelt at her feet and said in a choked voice, with tears in my eyes, Charlotte, marry me, I want to spend the rest of my life with you. I gave her the little box with the diamond ring. She looked at the ring and burst out laughing. She said, José, are you crazy? What we have is a fling. Besides which, I'm married and love my husband. This is just a weekly diversion, like going to the movies. José, forgive my saying this, but you're boring me, now you've taken to crying and I can't stand a man who cries. Charlotte then stopped laughing and said, very seriously: Another thing, I don't want to see you again.

I begged, sobbing, Charlotte, for the love of God, don't leave me. She patted me on the head as if I were a dog, turned her back, and left. I never saw her again. I lost the will to live.

Giselle, I ask forgiveness of you and our daughter for my act, but life without Charlotte is impossible. The box beside this letter contains the diamond ring that she refused. Good-bye, José.

Giselle tore up the letter, threw the wadded-up pieces into the toilet, and flushed it, several times. It was the end of the story. She didn't look at José's dead body for a long time. She stood there contemplating the diamond ring.

Tableau Vivant

Today we had a class on sexual drive. What is the nature of sexual drive? asked the professor. He wore glasses and his hair was greasy, he was utterly lacking in charm, and I don't think he could ever sexually motivate a woman. Predictably, he started to talk about Freud, reciting one of those canned phrases—sexuality is a powerful motivating force in human behavior. After listening to him go on about Freud, guys get off on Freud, I raised my hand and asked, what is sexual drive?

I liked to needle him. He detested me but I've caught him looking at my legs several times. Modesty aside, I have very good legs, I wear short skirts and when I sit down, I make sure to show them off. Irritated by my impertinent question and my interruption of his speech on Freud, the professor answered that sexual drive is dependent on a combination of internal and external factors, and he began to talk about hormones, brain function, and environmental stimuli. He even mentioned castration and its effects. Once again I interrupted him saying that the best product of castration was good male sopranos, as was the custom in antiquity.

When I left class, I got on the wrong subway train because I was reading the book assigned for class, which said something like this: In human beings cultural learning plays an important role in determining which characteristics one finds attractive in another person; anthropological studies show that the concept of feminine beauty varies in time and space; in some societies thin women are more valued, in others fat women are preferred. However, the statement that irritated me most was that the increase or decrease in attraction of the male also depended on the female's performance in bed. This always leaves me indignant—this really is a man's world. And what about our tastes, the sexual preferences of women? Don't they count? What about our thoughts, our fantasies, our dreams? Because, contrary to what happens with men, who focus just on a woman's physical attributes, our dreams and fantasies are a strong stimulant.

I only realized I had gotten on the wrong train when we were at 190th Street. Knowing I was near the Cloisters made me want to visit the museum, with its lovely tapestries, to contemplate the Hudson from its heights and appreciate its ancient architecture. However, I looked at the time and saw that I was late for work.

When I got there, the boss remarked, late again, eh? Get on your uniform, make it snappy.

I don't like anyone rushing me, I can't think. I took off my hat; I always wear a hat in the cold so that my body heat does not escape through my head. In the summer I wear one to protect myself from the sun. I unwound the scarf from my neck and folded it. Then I took off my overcoat and the rest of my clothing. I stowed it in my locker and put on my horrible uniform, a moss-green dress made of a cheap fabric. Who would think? Moss green, where have you ever seen that? I pinned up my hair without looking in the mirror, I didn't want to see myself in that color. I only feel really good wearing black or red. Strong colors. Well, that's not totally true. I also like blue, yellow, orange, pink, white, and violet. I like all colors, except moss green.

My first customer of the day was a round-faced guy with a bow tie and an alligator briefcase. I felt like telling him it was a crime to slaughter animals to make briefcases for idiots like him. But he would tell me that today there are alligator farms so that they can make briefcases for idiots. So I said nothing, just took his order. Later, when I put his plate on the table, the guy said in an Irish accent—or was it Australian?—that's not what I asked for, cheeseburger with fries and a beer, I asked for a club sandwich with ginger ale.

I thought he was messing with me because of my accent. He pronounced "club sandwich" like a Puerto Rican. I answered, what's your *problema*? Everything in this joint is *perfecto*. Eat your lunch and don't give me a hard time.

He was a nasty character, I could tell by his piggy eyes, and he asked me to call the manager. I refused. He got up and started yelling, who is the manager, where is the manager? Long story short, I was fired. The manager said that he couldn't keep me on, I was always late, this was the third time this week I had mixed up the orders, in addition to trying to force customers to eat what they hadn't ordered. I didn't try to apologize.

That's how life is, as much as people deny it. We always get what we wish for, even if what we wish for isn't good for us. I don't think that things happen by chance, we make chance happen. I had done everything I could to get fired, even though I needed the job. Why did I always get on the wrong train, arrive late, and insult the customers? It's because I didn't want to work in that dump. I felt like a slave. I even invented a nickname for myself: *cucaracha*. I was penniless and happy as a lark. If you have nothing, you have everything.

I started to spend more time on my studies and on my friends. I visited a classmate, Safira, who had been in an accident. She had tripped and fallen on the street, breaking a leg, and for a month all she could do was roll around in a wheelchair. What I am about to say may seem like an exaggeration, but it's the truth. I would rather die than become crippled. Imagine being dependent on others, pushed around in a wheelchair on the sidewalks! Maybe Safira was more intelligent or weaker than I; she smiled and talked as I pushed her around the city. I was more uncomfortable with her situation than she was.

It was clear that her accident had happened on purpose. I didn't say that to her face, I didn't want to scare her. I gathered up my courage and said, Safira, your accident was unconsciously premeditated, and I don't know if you are aware of this, but you wanted to hurt yourself, to have a reason not to go on with your life. This accident was a call for help, you must be going through a hard time, you must be confused, I don't know, only you can tell, I can't guess and I'm afraid how this might turn out.

Safira took my hand and said, you're right, Isabel. At this point we were sitting in Central Park, I was on a bench and she was in a wheelchair. I noticed she was about to cry, her face was red.

I never insist on prying, I never ask questions, that's how people open up, when we show a certain disinterest. By nature human beings want to share their torments, but first they need to be certain they can confide in us before they open up. And once they open up to release their emotional reservoir it's almost impossible to make them shut up.

To make a long story short, Safira really had contemplated suicide but what gave her the most trouble was that she didn't understand the reason for her despair. She admitted that she really wanted to fall on the street, she had thought of throwing herself in front of a bus, but she lost her nerve.

In six meetings with Safira I was able to solve her problem.

I know how to listen; I have the life skills, experience, capacity, and availability to understand people. Nothing goes by me unnoticed, nothing at all. I understand body language and silence. You need more sense and intelligence to understand a person's silences than to understand the sounds that she makes, words, coughs, throat clearings, all of which is easy. I read somewhere that learning the grammar of silence is more difficult than learning the grammar of sounds. There is an Irish proverb that says: a silent mouth sings melodies. I believe that. The same way that I believe that silence is as profound as eternity. Speech is as flat as time. And the most important thing: I never judge and I always understand. I will never try to perfect anyone, free them completely from their ghosts. Perfection, most of the time, leads to destruction. For that reason, my instinct is not to force anyone to discover their essential truth.

I am brave. Who at my age would leave a comfortable situation in their homeland to venture to another country? Many call me a compulsive liar. Yes, I do lie. But I also tell the truth. I am still a virgin at age twenty-nine. I take enormous pride in being a virgin, when nobody over twelve is anymore. Being a virgin is a way of being original.

Safira became the lover of the owner of a luxury restaurant and got me a job as a hostess.

A tall man of indeterminate age and geometrical features, inquisitive eyebrows, and almond-shaped eyes framed by rectangular designer glasses frequented the restaurant and would exchange a few words with me when he came in and when he left. He was always well-dressed in expensive clothes.

One night he said he would like me to work for him. He thought I seemed like a sensitive person. I asked what type of work. He said it was something connected to the senses, to our most basic impulses, to the pleasure of the mind and of the body. His eyes sparkled when he handed me his card, which was in very good taste. I could tell by the typeface and the quality of the paper. The name on the card was George Russo.

I figured that what he was offering me must be something transgressive, probably lecherous. I trusted him, after all he hadn't tried to deceive me, and he was being candid. I called George Russo the next day. He answered the phone. I listened attentively to each word, each pause, and each silence. His proposal was that I participate in a live sex show. I decided to meet with him to satisfy my curiosity.

For this meeting I decided to make myself up in a way that emphasized my resemblance to Pola Negri. We are very much alike; I am taller—she was a petite woman about five feet tall. I don't have the mole under my left eye, but I had it tattooed on as an adolescent. It's clear that my life could not be as adventurous as hers, she seduced Rudolf Valentino, she was the fiancée of Charles Chaplin and Hitler's lover, even though she was a Polish Jew. There's a saying of hers that has guided my life: "Love is disgusting if we are not our own master." I know that I'll die just like she did, of a brain tumor.

Pola Negri would not take a subway, that's why I went to the meeting by cab, dressed in black, trying out in front of my tiny purse mirror an enigmatic expression and a mysterious smile, just like hers.

George greeted me in one of the suites at the Astoria Hotel. After we made small talk, I told him I was an actress. Excellent, he said, since your work in the Théâtre d'Afrodite will be to act.

The Théâtre d'Afrodite consisted of the following: two or three women on a stage performed all the sexual acts that lesbians do to satisfy their libido, including using a vibrator, beads, and other paraphernalia. I would earn a good amount of money each time I participated. I explained I would do everything, except permit the introduction of anything into my vagina. I did not explain the reason for these terms. He agreed. He clarified that the theater was secret, confidential, that people who went there were high class. The audience sat in ten theater boxes, where they could eat, drink, fuck, in complete privacy.

It wasn't difficult to overcome my scruples. I accepted for one reason. When Safira had broken her leg, one day her mother could not bathe her because she had an appointment and she asked me to do it. I helped Safira out of bed, assisted her to the bathroom and had her sit on the toilet while I removed her clothing down to her panties. I was surprised; she was even more beautiful than I'd thought. Her breasts were just the right size; they were firm with small pink areolas. Her waist was slender and she did not have a belly. When I took off her panties I got excited at the sight her pubic area and its seductive smell. I took the brace off her leg. Safira invited me into the shower with her.

We both got into the shower. I soaped up my hands and began to rub soap on Safira's shoulders. There was a moment when my breasts brushed against her smooth, soft skin. A jolt went through my body. Carefully I turned her around to face me. When I soaped her breasts, her belly, and her pubic area she looked at me with desire. I felt an urge to kiss her, but I controlled myself. I grabbed a towel and dried her off without looking at her. That night I masturbated thinking about Safira, regretting I hadn't gone all the way. For that reason, I decided to repeat that unfinished experience. It wasn't the money that interested me, although George Russo was offering a decent amount. For three days we rehearsed a "tableau vivant" based on a painting by Ingres.

On the day of the performance I felt a shiver of excitement, a mixture of fear and euphoria. Playing on stage with me was Joyce, a very pretty young woman with long blond hair and golden skin. Before the curtain rose we assumed our positions. I lay down naked on a gray rug, reclining voluptuously on a striped cushion. My body faced the audience and my face was turned toward Joyce, who was positioned behind me. My arms were folded over my head in an asymmetrical and languid fashion. A diaphanous veil partially covered my legs. I wore a small chain around my neck, a bracelet on each arm, and a wavy auburn wig that flowed to a feather fan next to a hookah on the floor. Joyce wore a red-and-white turban on her head that hid her hair; she had a rope necklace wound three times around her neck, and a cobalt-blue tunic over two other tunics. She carried a lute that she fingered with a contemplative air. Jonny, the call boy, who was also in the tableau, was a well-built black guy, dressed in a white turban and an embroidered robe that fell to the floor. He stood motionless in the shadows, behind a wooden balustrade. He wore an invisible earphone, waiting for instructions from the director, George Russo himself.

Jonny whispered, quiet girls, don't move. It's show time. I had the impression of hearing champagne corks pop in the theater boxes. George Russo announced in a dramatic voice: Ladies and gentlemen, the tableau vivant that you are about to see is a representation of *L'odalisque à l'esclave*, by Jean-Auguste Dominique Ingres, the great neoclassical French painter, born 1780, died 1867.

With all that talk my boss was clearly trying to give an artistic and cultural veneer to all the pornography that was to follow. Russo's voice continued: Ingres was a perfection-ist; he tried to recreate on the canvas the textures and varied nuances of the colors of the fabrics and the skin of the orien-tal models that he portrayed as odalisques. You will see one of them now, in flesh and blood. (I felt like shouting, you cretin, Ingres never went to the Far East and the odalisques he painted were copied from engravings made by other art-ists, but I kept quiet.)

The velvet curtain started to rise slowly to the exotic sound of *Mozart in Egypt*, by Mozart and Courson. Joyce and I remained immobile. Then a voice ordered: action. Almost in slow motion, Joyce placed the lute on the floor and took off her turban. A cascade of curls fell over her shoulders. Then she started to take off her clothes piece by piece until she was entirely nude. Never had a woman's nudity impressed me so much. We had not undressed during our rehearsals.

Joyce knelt by my side and removed the transparent veil that covered my legs. I felt her tongue on my feet, then my ankles, on my knees, my inner thighs and my stomach. Her tongue lingered on my breasts in their dizzying caress. I forgot I was on a stage. She kissed my mouth, running her tongue on my lips and then her tongue on my tongue, and she sucked the saliva from my mouth in a long draw that took away my breath. My head, which has always been a bit confused, with thousands of thoughts weaving together with others in a tumultuous jumble, suddenly felt clear. When Joyce began to lick my vagina, a heat I had never felt took over my head and my body. I noticed it did the same thing to Joyce. The orgasm I experienced was like a liberating fire that made me shout. I returned to reality when I heard the applause and the voice of a woman exclaiming, *bravo*! *Bravissimo*! The curtain fell.

The person who helped me off the floor, where I was lying in a daze, was George Russo. He pulled me up by the arm, kissed each of us on the cheek, and put his arm around my shoulder. He said that he would meet me in my dressing room in five minutes to discuss something.

I took off my makeup, put on my jeans and T-shirt, and when I was putting on my sneakers I heard a knock on the door. It was Russo, with a box wrapped as a present. This is for you, doll. When I started to open the present, he interrupted, saying, not now, because one of the most important men in the country is waiting for you in his box. He looked around to make sure nobody was listening and he whispered a name I didn't catch, and even if I had it would have meant nothing because I wouldn't have known who it was. I don't read newspapers or watch television.

George Russo took me to the door of the theater box. He did not go in with me. A couple greeted me. I saw they were vainly conscious of their appearance. He was dressed all in black. He was tall, with healthy skin, without apparent wrinkles, and had well-cut gray hair. The woman wore a long bottle-green gown and a necklace of diamonds and emeralds. I could see from her face that she'd had plastic surgery. The man kissed my hand and said, this is my wife. The woman smiled, stepped up to me, and kissed my lips.

I don't know why, but that shocked me. I didn't know how to react. Me, who always knew what to say, who thought I knew it all, and who thought I understood everything. Perplexed, I said, I have to make a call. Use my cell phone, the woman said. No, I mumbled, I have to look up the number in my planner. I'll be right back.

I went to the dressing room, picked up my stuff, and left. I went on foot, walking for hours. By the time I got home, I was calm. I noticed I was carrying the present from the pseudo George Russo, whose real name was Dimitrius something or other. I unwrapped the present. It was a music box with the caption "Magic Dildo." It had a pale pink penis in the middle, activated by a button that turned on a red light and made the gland turn, while playing Strauss's "Blue Danube Waltz."

I threw the thing out the window and watched it break apart on the street. Predictably, it was made in China.

I took off my clothes and went to bed.

The Vice

The last few times I spent the night at Bettina's place, a small part of my left hand, just below the little finger, known in palmistry as the Mount of Mars, broke into a clammy sweat moments before we put out the light to go to sleep. Whenever that happened, weak laughter would take hold of me. Bettina would ask the cause of the laughter. "Beats me," I'd say. It was true; I didn't exactly know the reason.

One night I started laughing that same laugh when Bettina, forgetting to turn off the light, had already fallen asleep. Still lying in bed, I looked up. Jesus was pinned on a cross on the wall behind my head. He was abstract and made of wood, so was the cross. I identified him because the only person I know of who was nailed to a wooden cross is him. Bettina must have hung it there to protect her. Would that wooden Jesus also preserve me from the discomforts and dangers of life?

I didn't think about that for much longer, as it didn't interest me. I was more concerned that the sweat on my left hand continued, staying the same size. The only factor that varied was the intensity.

That was the first time I suffered from total insomnia after making love to Bettina, who left me exhausted. She was a tireless woman, she claimed that after knowing many men, she had finally achieved orgasm with me. I don't know if she was lying to please me, but it didn't matter. It was good to hear her say it. She also said my dick was the largest she'd ever seen. She even measured it with a ruler.

The sweat on my hand was increasing; I couldn't manage to sleep. An eerie feeling of isolation took over my soul. I couldn't stay there, with that woman. Something not so unknown was revealing itself to me, something that I still didn't understand exactly, but I could feel it clearly. It was insisting, once again, on something that was destroying me.

Bettina represented everything I had always hated. True, she was a very pretty woman and had a face with fine features and a well-shaped body, but one practically covered with tattoos; only her ass was white. Within limits, because she had bikini lines, another thing that I disliked. It wasn't just that; Bettina's breasts were fake. Not to mention that she didn't work, never had worked, and had no intention of working. I have nothing but disgust for bums and spoiled women. Worst of all was the fact of Bettina preventing me from working. She demanded all my time, and, as I'm self-employed, it was a disaster. For months I'd done nothing, merely dedicated myself to her. I was in love. My hand was sweating.

That very night, when we were fucking for the second time, Bettina turned over, face down, and I got on top of her, and as always found myself facing that colored snake tattooed on her back. The snake's tail started in her lower lumbar region and the drawing of the animal ran all the way up her spine to the nape of her neck, where the phrase Welcome to Hell came from the serpent's open mouth. I bit Bettina's neck, bit that phrase. I thought I was going to go limp, but to my relief she came and we stopped there. Actually, I did go limp, but she didn't notice and fell asleep right away. I sat there looking at that beautiful body, all painted and stretched out on the sheet.

That was when my hand started to sweat. I looked at Jesus Christ and remembered the phrase Welcome to Hell. I had read that phrase frequently on Bettina's neck, but that night for some reason I felt a kind of panic. As if for an instant I had no idea what I was doing there. Could I be in hell?

I sat up on the edge of the bed, rested my elbows on my knees, and put my head in my hands. I reflected. My thoughts were composed of imperfect, even rhetorical digressions. My loneliness seemed to be accentuated in that bedroom. I couldn't go on there. Bettina would wipe out my life. It was like some kind of curse. I couldn't even manage to look at other women. I was never faithful; no matter how much in love I was I always liked women and never resisted the charms of those creatures. I would go out with one, with two, with three. The only time I went to bed with someone else while I was with Bettina, I experienced terrible guilt. I felt no pleasure and left as fast as I could. I made up some excuse.

I don't consider myself a philanderer. I was always very loyal to my wives. Screwing different women is a separate pleasure, independent of any marriage. It's a virtue, and anyone who possesses it feels obliged to exercise it. I'm a fucker, but I never neglected my women. I've been married three times. I always chose docile women who had things to do and left me alone. They didn't try to take over my life. Even going out with other women during those marriages, I never stopped liking them, fucking them, and meeting my obligations as a husband. I have two daughters, one with my first wife and another who was born from the third union. They say that every really promiscuous man has daughters, to teach him a lesson. My three marriages ended . . . I don't know the exact reason, but I suspect it's because I've always had vices.

I sometimes think I'm sick, because I do everything in excess. I've sought treatment, and I've gotten rid of my other vices, but I made up for them with sex. Sex, in a way, allowed me to work. With Bettina it was impossible. I no longer took a step without telling her, and if she needed me I would cancel any commitment to be at her side. And she required me at every instant. Bettina would finally crush me. That was exactly the word I thought, crush. I knew it was a shameful situation, so much so that I didn't have the courage to introduce her to my family. In the middle of that night I made a discovery: I was addicted to Bettina. That had never happened to me, becoming addicted to only one woman. And what a woman, a tattooed woman who existed in the void. It was easier to blame her for those uncontrollable, compulsive feelings of mine. And that's what I did.

Resolute, I got up and said, "Wake up, I'm leaving and won't be coming back. It's over."

Saying this produced an indescribable feeling of pleasure in me. So I repeated: "I'm leaving. You hear, I'm leaving. It's over."

Bettina looked at me solemnly, not saying a word.

"Aren't you going to say anything?" She remained silent, stretched out in the bed. I raised my voice and a feeling of freedom made me begin to shout. I said how much I detested her way of being, how she suffocated me, stifled me. That her dedication left me with a sensation of debt. How could I, I asked aloud, obey a tattooed, idle woman? "How?" I screamed. "How? Go ahead. Say something."

Bettina continued mute, staring at me. I stopped talking, because in a way I was waiting for some reaction on her part.

I thought she was going to cry, ask for explanations, say she loved me, but no, she remained immobile. I gestured with my head, as if to say, speak. Bettina didn't react. In light of this, I had no other option. "Don't you have anything to say to me?"

"Yes," she answered. "You can leave."

I stood there frozen, as if I hadn't understood. She couldn't live without me. I continued without moving, hoping she would change her mind. But she remained silent. I got dressed slowly, hoping she would reconsider. When I finished putting on my shoes, I looked at her in the bed. I realized that Bettina wasn't going to say anything, and that produced in me a weakness that I had long tried to conceal. I felt like crying but couldn't. My pride wouldn't let me. I turned my back and left, hating the woman.

I walked the streets, determined to rid my mind of Bettina.

But I couldn't. I've had every kind of vice, but this was the worst of all.

I went back to the apartment. Bettina was still in bed.

"What took you so long?" she asked.

Tocata and Fugue

You could call it sexual perversion. That's beside the point. The only thing that matters is the pleasure it gives me. Some can in fact say that I should be ashamed of this situation. I am not ashamed.

I'm a hedonist, I'm Catholic, I'm full of contradictions, and what I'm really good at is being myself and that's enough.

I've already tried to understand why I seek this type of pleasure, I don't know why, I don't understand it, and that's exactly why I enjoy it.

I think it's important to stress that I had a happy childhood, I never suffered corporal punishment from my parents, nor was I abandoned or molested, as they like to invent to justify my behavior.

I remember that Sérgio used to kiss me on the neck and then one time his teeth accidently brushed my skin. I said, I like it when you bite me, and he answered, I didn't bite you. You can bite me, I like it. Then he bit me on the neck and kissed my belly until he got to my breasts. I murmured in his ear, bite me, bite me, I begged, bite me hard. He bit me, leaving tooth marks on my nipple.

Another day we were making love and I whispered, hit me. He didn't understand, and I repeated, hit me. Confused, Sérgio said, what? I shouted, hit me! How? he asked. I answered, with your hands. Still incredulous, he questioned, where? In the face, my face, I said. He hit me, my body trembled, I succumbed to pleasure. Harder, I shouted. He slapped me, my face burned, I moaned, he grabbed me by the hair, I came in his arms and passed out on the bed. Sérgio fell on me with all his weight and came.

When Sérgio and I were going out, on the few occasions that we made love we listened to Bach. *Gloria Patri, Gloria Filio, Gloria et Spiritui Sancto. Sicut erat in principio, et nunc, et semper, et in saecula saeculorum. Amen.* Afterward he worshipped me with blows and bites. That music was my music.

I forgot to say my name is Glória. The next day I looked at myself in the mirror, with the *Magnificat* playing in the background, and it was joyously trumpeting my name, Glória. The next day I examined my sore body, each bruise, each bite mark. I knew I was happy.

One night I asked Sérgio to take me on the dining room table, which was round and small. The table toppled over and we both ended up on the floor. I felt a sharp pain in my hip. Sérgio took me to the hospital. I had broken my iliac bone.

I was prepped for surgery and when I returned to my room, still groggy from the anesthesia, I had a very pleasant dream. I dreamed about the Cathedral of Murcia, that centuries-old construction, with its ninety-five-meter tower that seemed to touch the sky. The entrance was framed in a great, elaborately sculpted baroque façade, ornamented with columns and abundant reliefs. In my dream I glided into the cathedral, attracted by the organ music, Bach's *Tocata and Fugue*, playing in the interior. I stopped, overcome with wonder. Then I walked through the nave of the church, sat in a pew in silence, kneeled, and without praying, I felt the presence of God.

Sérgio visited me every day in the hospital. He sat in a chair next to my bed, he took care of me, he felt responsible for the accident. I couldn't move, I was at his mercy. Dependent on the man who was protecting me, I agreed to marry him, even though reason told me that it was an impulsive act. I said from my hospital bed, yes, I want to be your wife.

We got married as soon as I was better. As I have already said, I am very Catholic, I've always believed that marriage is a lifelong commitment. I made a point of getting married in the church.

After the religious ceremony, we hosted a reception for

our friends. Sérgio drank too much. We went to a hotel and on the next day we left for a honeymoon in Porto. Since the event that landed me in the hospital, we hadn't had any great intimacy. We started kissing, he took off my clothes, we got naked, we lay down and Sérgio started to enter me. I whispered in his ear, hit me, hit me, and I had the impression that he let out a soft sigh, then he rolled off me, lay down beside me, and said, I'm sorry, my love, I drank too much during the reception. Perturbed, I turned away from him and pretended to fall asleep. A few minutes later I heard his snoring. That was the first time I heard him snore. Maybe because on the few occasions we had spent the night together I had fallen asleep right after making love.

We awoke and hurried to the airport. The flight was delayed and we sat in the waiting room. Going to Porto was a cause of great happiness for me, after all, it's the city where the expressive Baroque architecture manifests itself in innumerable civic and religious buildings. I wanted to show Sérgio that side of Portugal, a country I know very well, since I lived there for three years when I was studying at the University of Coimbra for my Master's in Art History, with a specialization in the Baroque.

While we waited for the plane, I told my husband that we would see the splendid church of the Convent of Santa Clara, where we could appreciate the gilt and polychrome work of one of the best interpreters of the Joanina Baroque, the painter Miguel Francisco da Silva.

Sérgio looked at me with a distant expression, he didn't react, not even a sign of boredom, it was as if he didn't hear me. I asked if he knew the Santa Clara Church and he said, that so? That so what, Sérgio? I'm sorry, dear, I got distracted. And I fell silent.

When we boarded the plane, the first thing he did was to pull out the on-board magazine to look at the film listings. We took off and he watched one movie after the other through the entire flight, even during meals. It was obvious that he didn't want to talk with me, he was so embarrassed about what had happened the night before.

From Lisbon we went on to Porto. Sérgio asked me to tell him what we would be doing in Porto. I answered that we would visit the house of Canon Domingos Barbosa and the Church of the Order of the Rosary, with its façade of carved granite, displaying elements of the Rococo, and an interior decorated with ornately painted plaster and wooden carvings. Next to this church was the Hospital of Our Lady of the Rosary and Charity, which is a jewel of the Baroque. I told Sérgio that I wouldn't mind being a patient in that hospital, that I would be happy in there even if I were dying. He said I was being morbid. Sérgio didn't understand my sense of humor. I grew quiet again.

It was getting late; we went straight to the hotel, since the trip had been tiring. We took a bath, ordered sandwiches from room service, and lay down. In bed I tried to stimulate him by kissing and touching him. Before he would always get excited, but now there was no reaction. Sérgio apologized saying he didn't know what was going on. I tried several times in the following days, with no results. Our honeymoon continued in that fashion, we didn't make love once.

I sensed that because he was feeling awkward, he tried to please me by asking me to talk about the Baroque. One day I talked about music. I explained that Baroque music was intimately related to the life of the church and the court and that, progressively, sacred music became dramatic and secular.

He listened to me quietly and attentively. He said he preferred to stay in the room listening to me rather than visiting the museums and Baroque monuments. He still liked to go out to the restaurants, and he always drank too much.

The next day I commented on Baroque literature. I told Sérgio that from the aesthetic point of view, the Baroque presents a constant search for novelty; the attraction to difficulty, tied to the tendency to artifice and ingenuity. I explained that Baroque literature is characterized by the use of dramatic language expressed in exaggerated devices such as hyperbole, metaphor, anacoluthon, and antithesis.

Sérgio remained horizontal on the bed while I talked. I confess I was getting a bit irritated; I wanted to go out to see cathedrals. He said he wouldn't accompany me, he was tired and he told me I should visit the churches alone. We ate lunch in the room and then I went out without him.

When I returned, Sérgio was completely drunk. I hated the smell of alcohol on his breath when I was near him. I got dressed and we went out to dinner. In the restaurant he behaved inappropriately, he argued loudly with the waiter, saying he had asked for whiskey with ice, but in fact I had clearly heard him ask for it neat. It was a relief to return to the hotel. He fell into bed and started snoring. I don't know if I was being too critical but it seemed that Sérgio's snoring kept getting louder.

I slept badly. I woke up depressed, knowing that not even the most beautiful cathedral would relieve my distress, just one thing could make me happy: shopping. Sérgio, learning of my intentions, said sarcastically that I had taken my time unleashing my consumer proclivities.

I wanted to buy several things. A handbag, maybe two. In one of the stores I looked at three bags, but I couldn't decide. I ended up buying all three. I'm crazy about purses. It's almost an obsession.

In the best shoe store, after two hours of trying on innumerable styles of sandals, boots, spike heels, flats, and moccasins, I ended up buying black spike pumps, closed in the front and with open heels, and leather straps that tied around the ankles. I also bought a pair of red flats with little crystal appliqués. They were a little tight but of such delicate beauty that I couldn't resist them.

In an elegant dress shop I found a pure silk print dress

with tiny blue and violet flowers. I tried it on, it had to be mine. I bought it.

Arriving at the hotel with my arms full of shopping bags, I found Sérgio sitting in front of the TV with a glass of whiskey in his hand. He hadn't even changed from the pajamas he was wearing when we had breakfast. Seeing my packages, he said in a mildly irritated voice, I see you bought a shitload of unnecessary stuff that's going to mildew in the closet. I didn't respond. We ate dinner in the room. As soon as we finished, Sérgio returned to the television. A little later I noticed he had fallen asleep with his mouth open. I didn't wake him. I went to bed to read and a little while later I fell asleep.

When I got up in the morning, Sérgio was still sleeping in front of the television. It was still on. I tugged at his arm and said softly, Sérgio, come with me, you're going to take off those pajamas and take a bath.

After he was bathed and shaved, Sérgio felt better and suggested we eat breakfast in the hotel bar. During breakfast I told him that last night I read an interesting book about Baroque painting. It was about the works of Caravaggio, Rembrandt, and Vermeer; their works could be seen in museums not far from where we were staying. From Portugal we can catch a plane and get to those museums in no time.

Sérgio exclaimed, what? What? We're going to take a plane? I didn't want to go as far as the corner to see that church you talked about and now you want to take a plane. You insisted we come here and now you want to go somewhere else? What for? To see more Baroque? Haven't you noticed that you're a bore, showing off your academic knowledge, wanting to seem like an intellectual, an expert? This is ridiculous; nobody is interested in your shitty Baroque.

We ate breakfast in silence. When we were finished, I told Sérgio I had to exchange some of the things I'd bought yesterday. He told me to go ahead.

The truth was, I wasn't going to exchange anything. I just wanted to be alone. I needed to think. I wandered around the streets with no particular destination in mind, not even window shopping. I kept walking and then noticed I was back at the hotel.

When I walked into the room, I'd made a decision: we would return early to Brazil. Sérgio accepted my suggestion, but he said, you have to deal with the travel agency. Two days later we returned to Brazil.

I wasn't at peace but I also didn't have the will or the courage to make any decisions. An unease settled over me, as if nothing made sense anymore. I looked at that house, the color of the walls, the pictures still to be hung, the furniture, and objects that hadn't even been used, the still wrapped wedding presents. I couldn't give everything up so fast; I had to make one last try.

I went to the bedroom. Sérgio was on the bed watching television. I lay down next to him and embraced him. He put his arms around me and kissed me. I said, I love you, he answered, I love you too. I said that trying to convince myself that I loved him, as if by using that phrase could revive my love for him. But the truth was, I had never loved him.

It was worse to have said it. He said that he loved me too, and that made me sad.

Without looking at each other, we started to kiss. He kissed my throat and started to take off my blouse, and then he kissed my breasts. I asked him to bite me. He did not react. He kept kissing me. I asked again, please, bite me. He kissed me on the mouth and penetrated me. I said, hit me. He didn't react. Hit me, hit me please, I said. He pushed me away, withdrew from me and said, that's enough!

Sérgio got dressed. He left the room. I also got dressed and went after him. In the living room I approached him and asked, what's going on? Irritated, he answered, I don't like to do that stuff, it makes me uncomfortable. But we did it before, I answered. But it was a mistake, he shouted. I asked, then why did you ask me to marry you after we did what you said was a mistake? Sérgio said, it was out of pity, I thought I had crippled you.

That's how our marriage ended. I'm single, I wear glasses, and in spite of having given up any amorous involvement, I haven't gotten fat. I wrote a book about Baroque art, it was a big success. I teach at the university and I am considered one of the greatest specialists in the Baroque in our country. I'm happy, or at least I believe I'm happy and that life has given me everything I have ever wanted.

I keep going to Mass on Sundays. But when I see certain men, they aren't even good-looking, and I look at their large, thick hands, I feel a shiver run through my body.

New Year's Eve

December 31 had always been a happy day for João Paulo. The bustle of street vendors and the aroma of barbecue and melting cheese on the grill were perfume to his nostrils. It was clear that this New Year's Eve would be even better than last year.

The black plastic sack that João Paulo carried on his back was almost full; only four more cans would fit inside it. There was no need to make the effort to search for discarded cans, as he normally did during the course of the year. He crushed the can with his foot, flattening it as much as possible, because the flatter he got it, the more cans he could fit inside the sack. He crushed three more in succession. He tied a knot in the sack, slung it over his shoulder, and walked to the beach, where his eight-year-old son, Daniel, was waiting for him. Not far from Daniel on the beach, a group of *candomblé* worshippers sang to the sound of drumbeats around an altar of flowers and lit candles. João Paulo reached the spot where his son waited, and Daniel helped his father place the sack next to the others tied to a cart that João Paulo had recently purchased. Both father and son were proud of this acquisition. They had it custom-made at a little shop near their house. The cart had an iron frame covered by a wooden platform and two wheels with number 13 tires. The platform was nine feet long and twenty inches wide, and the cart could carry up to 110 pounds. Under the iron frame, João Paulo had installed a basket to carry personal items and food. As he prepared to collect more cans, João Paulo picked up an empty garbage bag and said, keep your eyes open, Daniel, there are a lot of bums around. Don't worry, Dad, leave it to me, said the boy. Good boy, the father replied.

As he walked toward the crowd, João Paulo felt proud. He was setting a good example for his son, he was working, he was a man of honor. He didn't beg, like the scum who wandered the streets asking for handouts. He would rather die than to humiliate himself by panhandling.

The streets and sidewalks were littered with beer and soda cans. The ground was full of bottles and paper as well, but these did not interest him. What a windfall, he exulted; there was one can after another, thousands littering the pavement. He felt like hugging and kissing the men and women in white, who drank raucously and tossed their cans to the ground. Brazilians are the happiest people on earth, he thought. It was not even midnight. He asked a policeman, what time is it, my friend? It was ten to midnight.

Before he had completely filled his sack, he returned to his son, Daniel, and told him, soon you'll see something you have never seen before. The crowd began to chant, ten, nine, eight, seven, six . . . Then an explosion illuminated the sky with a huge burst of light. The crowd went wild, people embraced, champagne corks popped, beer cans were peeled open, cans and bottles clanked together, and the revelers shouted "Happy New Year!" João Paulo hugged his son and gave him a kiss. The two stood looking at the scene, fascinated, awed by the showers of colored lights exploding in the sky. At that moment, they forgot about the recycled cans, the boy's sick mother, they forgot everything.

After the pyrotechnic display ended, the father said, I am going to collect more cans, take care of things, son.

The drunken crowd danced and sang, there were so many people that João Paulo had trouble picking up the cans from the ground. More than once as he crouched to retrieve one, he was pushed or jostled, sometimes people even stepped on his hands. But he was not deterred; he got up, crushed the can with his foot and dropped it in the sack. The only thing that irritated him was when after he'd crushed a can, someone would kick it far away from him, or worse, when they almost yanked off his sandals. That would have put him out of business since his feet were already swollen.

A stage on the beach was illuminated for the New Year's

Eve show. A mass of people huddled around, filling up the beach; shouts greeted the musicians when a loud, syncopated sound started to blare from the speakers. The show went on all night with a string of bands playing in succession. It only stopped when the sun began to rise.

João Paulo continued to collect the cans, filling sacks and taking them to Daniel. His legs and feet ached, but he did not relent, there were still many more to be found. When he returned with the last sack he saw that his son was stretched out on the sand, sleeping next to the cart. He shook the boy. Daniel, didn't I tell you to watch out for our things? The boy woke up frightened and said he was sorry. When we get home, said João Paulo, you can rest. We just have to tie up this load and we can go.

They tied up the sacks and João Paulo instructed his son to climb up on the cart. He lay down on the load of cans. It wasn't long before Daniel was asleep.

João Paulo felt like singing but he couldn't remember the words to any songs. So he whistled while he pulled his cart along behind him.

She and She

Her soft skin glided over mine. We were dancing, hesitant and laughing. It was delightful to be in a place where no one knew me, that's one of the best things about being a tourist. I was in a nightclub called The Pussy Cat. I don't know how I got there. Me and a girlfriend. After a few martinis, I was dancing, brushing against a woman I didn't know who called me darling. She was a bit taller than me, with a trim waist, muscular legs, large firm breasts, and bleached blond hair. We were dancing to any rhythm, our own rhythm, it didn't matter, techno was playing and any movement is in sync with that kind of music. Sweat covered our bodies, but strangely I wasn't disgusted when I pressed my body against hers. She grasped me by the hips and began grinding against me, her eyes closed, her pink-tinted lips half open. Without thinking, I slowly licked her lips, and she stuck her tongue in my mouth. I put both hands on her round breasts and squeezed them forcibly, then lowered one of my hands inside her panties, down to her pussy, which I discovered was wet. She was wearing a black Lurex miniskirt. We went on kissing, I had always wanted to kiss a woman and it had to be a stranger. Women I knew, my girlfriends, always inhibited me. She put her hand on my ass inside my jeans, I was over-come by the lack of air you only experience when you're really turned on. I wasn't looking for affection or tenderness, that was something I always expected from men. I wanted to use and be used by a woman. I wanted to fuck that stranger, that pussy, wanted to hear her moan, call me darling, amid sighs and moans. She had no face, no voice, no past, present or future, she had no name. I fucked her in the night club bathroom and then we went to her apartment, where I went on fucking her and she sucked me, went down on all fours, from the side, from the front, from the back. Then I got up, dressed, and left. I wandered in the street, I don't know where. And discovered how a man feels.

Settling Accounts

My father abandoned my mother months after I was born. So my mother and I had to move into the home of my maternal grandmother.

My mother had only one brother, Uncle Otávio, a failed economist who worked for an import firm for a pitiful salary. A friend of his was elected president of the nation and made him head of a large state entity, where he had the opportunity to get rich through corrupt measures, which allowed him to give his mother, my grandmother, a life of luxury. She was a born spender and came to love her favorite child even more. She traveled to Europe every year, staying in the best hotels, and would return loaded down with purchases, all for herself. She never brought me or my mother, who was after all her daughter, a single present.

With the money from his shady dealings my uncle bought a beautiful mansion where he lived with his wife Daniela, an extremely thin woman with a delicate, fragile face.

I began spending every weekend at that luxurious house. It had a pool, tennis court, volleyball court, a garage for several cars, a game room, a climate-controlled wine cellar with hundreds of bottles. He had almost no friends, an irascible man who fought with anyone who disagreed with him. We would spend the weekends practically by ourselves, me, Uncle Otávio, and Aunt Daniela. They had no children. Uncle Otávio had a playground built for me, with a swing, a slide, a dollhouse, countless toys, and he gave me a present that touched me deeply, a beautiful white puppy I named Snowflake but which ended up being known by the nickname Flaky.

I loved going there, and my uncle, in a certain way, played the role of my father. Whenever I arrived he would put me on his lap. He didn't call me by my name, Joanna, he called me "little princess." He was very affectionate. He would make up games, like hide-and-seek. He would ask me to dance for him by the pool while he filmed me. He was so tall, so good-looking, that I loved it when my friends saw him. I was proud of him, grasping his hand and pretending to everyone that he was my father.

When I was eight, more or less, I was lying down watching television wearing a long knit shirt and panties. Uncle Otávio came into the living room and lay down beside me. He hugged me and we watched a film. He began pulling me toward his body and kissed me in a different way. He ran his tongue along my neck and into my ear. I laughed and told him it tickled. He told me to close my eyes, because I would really like what he was about to do.

I obeyed and went on laughing a little. I was surprised

when I felt his hand between my legs, under my panties. I was frightened and kept my eyes tightly shut. A dark sensation that I was unable to understand overwhelmed me. What was he doing? Then Uncle Otávio picked me up and carried me to the bed, covered me with the sheet, kissed me on the forehead and said, "Good night, little princess." I couldn't get to sleep.

For several years, whenever I stayed at his house, he would come into my room, caress my body, my still non-existent breasts, my hairless vagina. I was certain that it was wrong because he only acted like that secretly. But it was good to have a secret that belonged just to the two us. I would pretend to be asleep, as if unaware of what was happening.

But after a time I began to feel tormented, I would remain rigid, my legs closed. I couldn't take any longer his caressing my body and doing all those things, but I wasn't yet ready to resist. He was the only person who did whatever I wanted, who protected me.

One night I spoke to him, begging him to stop. He kissed me on the forehead and said there was nothing wrong in it, it was just a way of showing affection. I felt his damp lips on my mouth and tried to push him away, but he grabbed me forcibly and got on top of me. He ripped off my panties and raped me.

I stopped going to his house. I thought that would let

me forget everything. But there are some things you never forget. I regretted not telling my mother right from the beginning, but I didn't have the courage and wouldn't have known how.

To make my pain worse, when I phoned Aunt Daniela to ask for Flakey, she said Uncle Otávio had found the puppy dead in the garden and thrown it in the garbage.

I was wasting away inside; I had almost no friends at school and spent the days locked in my room, drawing. On weekends I would stay by myself, often just staring at the wall. Until one day I told my mother everything. I wasn't able to give the details.

My mother told my grandmother what had happened. She replied that she didn't believe her dear generous son could do such a thing. She added that I was a problem child, an ungrateful little liar.

My mother resigned from the job that Uncle Otávio had gotten her. We had to move to a small one-bedroom apartment that my father had left us when he deserted us. I never again spoke to my grandmother. But I knew my mother met with her from time to time, always behind my back.

Mom found a job as a clerk in a dress shop, working only on commission. I started attending a public school. As soon as I turned sixteen I found work as a hostess at nights, in a restaurant.

Whenever I could, I would wander into the kitchen and watch the chef and his helpers as they worked. I asked one of them where he had learned to cook. "In a school funded by a commercial association," he replied. "I liked it a lot. It's free, and you even get a diploma." It was a two-year course. I asked him for the address.

I signed up for the cooking class at the free school. Classes met every day for three hours and included training the cook in the service routine and preparing Italian, Portuguese, Spanish, French, and Japanese cuisine in addition to typical Brazilian dishes. I also took a baking course, where besides bread and phyllo dough I learned to make sweet and savory dishes in general.

After graduating I went to work in another, more sophisticated restaurant. I began as a helper and in less than two years had become the right-hand assistant to the chef, a well-known Frenchman. I liked working there, but my dream was to open a restaurant of my own. To make that possible, my mother sold our apartment and bought one in a good location at a reasonable price. We painted it ourselves, made the tablecloths, worked till we dropped. We went to live in an old building with dozens of apartments per floor. It was a cubicle that didn't even have a stove, just a hotplate that sat on top of the sink built into the wall. We slept on a sofa bed.

Mom continued to work at the dress shop and me at

the restaurant. To help with the cooking I hired Aristides, who was from Ceará. A waitress named Chris helped me with serving. The restaurant had six tables and a set menu for each day of the week. We were open for lunch and dinner, which meant two menus a day. The restaurant became known in the neighborhood, and lines began forming at the entrance. The customers praised my cooking, whether it was a risotto, a paella, grilled cod, a bouillabaisse, or some typically Brazilian dish.

One day Aristides called me aside and whispered in a frightened voice that he had known the guy sitting at table three back in Ceará, a dangerous hired killer named Tião.

"What's the problem, Aristides?" I said.

"It's just that he saw me, Miss Joanna. He recognized me and made a gesture like he wanted to talk to me."

"Go over there, Aristides, and see what he wants."

Aristides went to speak to the guy and came back relieved. Tião merely wanted to praise the food and know if we served jerked beef with squash. "I told him, Miss Joanna, that we serve that dish, jerked beef with squash, every Thursday, at lunch."

And every Thursday, Tião, or *the killer*, as Aristides and I called him, would have lunch at the restaurant. Fortunately, he wasn't the only steady customer we'd attracted.

Suddenly, newspapers and magazines were talking about

our food. We had more customers than we could handle. We started taking reservations. It was a success. We worked day and night, but it didn't bother me. I was very happy, even if I didn't go out, see movies, or have a boyfriend. Everything was going as planned, even better. I was doing what I enjoyed, the restaurant was making money, and my mother and I could finally move to a decent apartment.

One night, at closing time, when we weren't accepting any more diners, I was in the kitchen with Aristides working on the next day's menu when Chris came in and said there was a gentleman who insisted on eating and was anxious to try the food. I asked if there was just one person. She said yes. I decided to let him in.

When I went to the dining room I experienced a surprise: it was Uncle Otávio. It had been almost fifteen years since we'd seen each other. But, as I've said before, certain things you never forget. He was different: short, old, and ugly. He looked at me and said, "A long time, eh, Princess?"

With difficulty, I repressed the disgust that threatened to overwhelm me and said, "Good evening, Uncle Otávio."

When I passed by his table again, he was on his second bottle of wine. He invited me to have a drink with him. We drank the wine in silence. Meanwhile, I was planning how to settle accounts.

Uncle Otávio, drunk, said in a thick voice, "Princess, you

haven't changed a bit, you look like that same little thirteen-year-old girl . . . You think we could get together?"

"Yes, but not today," I replied. "Leave your phone number with the waitress and I'll get in touch with you." I got up and hid in the kitchen.

I waited a week, then phoned him.

"Uncle Otávio," I said, "it's Joanna."

"Ah, Princess, at last. I can't sleep from thinking about you, I've got to see you, I want to be alone with you."

"Come by the restaurant," I said.

The next day, Uncle Otávio showed up at the restaurant, had dinner, and again asked me to sit with him. "When are we going to be alone together?" he asked.

"I promise we're going to, just be patient, Uncle Otávio. First, I'd like you to co-sign for a bank loan so I can expand my restaurant." Uncle Otávio looked at me pensively for a few moments. He knew that co-signing for the loan wasn't a problem; he'd become a millionaire through his thefts from the government.

"I'll do anything you want, Princess."

With the resources from the excellent bank loan for which Uncle Otávio had co-signed, I was able to open the restaurant I'd always wanted. The location was perfect. I remodeled everything. I had a state-of-the-art kitchen put in, and in the basement built a bakery for making pies and various pastries. I was the chef and had two sous-chefs, one of them Aristides. The hostess was a beautiful young woman, elegant and refined. Chris also went on working for me. Despite being on the pricey side, my restaurant was so popular that reservations had to be made well in advance. Only one person didn't need to make reservations: Tião, the killer.

Uncle Otávio was constantly calling me to ask, irritated, "So, are we getting together or not? Just the two of us."

"Take it easy," I said, "we are, any day now."

"Alone," he insisted. "You've been leading me on for too long."

As soon as the killer came into the restaurant, I went over to his table.

"Mr. Tião, is the jerked beef and squash to your liking?" He nodded. "May I sit down? I want to propose something." He gestured for me to join him at his table. He was a man of few words.

"I want you to kill someone." He nodded again, just a tiny movement of his head. "But I want that person to suffer terribly before dying, I want him to be tortured slowly."

Tião, still eating, again gestured his agreement. "When I open the newspaper one of these mornings, I want to read the news of that bastard's death. Then come by here and I'll pay your price. Do you want an advance?"

He didn't want payment until the job was done. I handed him an envelope with Uncle Otávio's photo and address.

Three days later, leafing through the morning paper, I saw the headline: "Tortured and murdered." There was a picture of Uncle Otávio and the report began: "The naked and mutilated body of the well-known businessman Otávio Morais was found in an empty lot in the Baixada Fluminense. Forensic experts say he was subjected to a lengthy process of torture." I didn't read the rest.

I went to the wake, early in the morning. Uncle Otávio's body was in the casket, with no one around. We were finally alone, just as he wanted, but in the way I had chosen.

The account was settled.

The next morning, I went to a pet shop to buy a puppy. I took him away in my arms. He was pure white. Holding the puppy, I walked down the street, free and cleansed. I looked at the sky. It was noon, a day with neither clouds nor shadows.

The Laughing Assassin

You're not just stuck up, you're stupid too. Before you mess around with a man who already belongs to a woman, you should find out who she is. But you were in such a hurry to give him pussy that you didn't think. Or worse, you thought the wrong thing. You were thinking what? That Cosmo would leave me for you? That you were going to fuck him in my bed and I would put up with it? I won't stand for lack of respect, you little shit. When I saw you leaving here from my house, I remembered your pretty little face. And revenge, as Cosmo taught me, is a dish you eat cold. So, you're going to learn never again to mess around with a man who has a woman and Cosmo will have to learn how to respect me. Sit still there, it's no use whining or asking my pardon. I'm not a woman you can mess with. He might be out there fucking around but if I find out, the nigger will have to pay for it. Don't worry, I'm not going to kill you. You're going to become an example for other hos so they think twice before they get involved with my man. I love my Cosmo and I'm not in the mood to share him with anybody. Cosmo made me into the woman I am today and I'm capable of crazy shit just to keep him for myself. When Cosmo met me I was a maid, that's right, I washed pots and pans and toilets in the madam's house. I only got off on Saturday afternoons and Mondays I had to wake up at four in the morning to arrive at the boss lady's house at seven in the morning, so she'd have fresh rolls when she got up. Fresh rolls and the table set for breakfast, with orange juice and those little cheese balls that she liked but didn't let me eat. But one Saturday, Deborah, my cousin, took me to a dance. It was there, at the Brazilian Funk, that I met Cosmo. Love at first sight. I was eighteen. I knew right away that Cosmo would be my man. He came over to talk to me, brought me a beer. I refused because I don't drink. He could tell I was a serious woman. Cosmo doesn't like a lush. And we started to go out. The next day he went to my house to meet my family. He was polite, a gentleman, he picked me up at work so we could go to the beach. One day he said to me, you're my woman and I don't want you to keep working for those society bitches. I left my job and went to live with Cosmo. God looks out for me and is looking out for me now. Looking out for you too, you slut. And what are you thinking? God is on my side. He said, don't covet your neighbor's wife. But this goes for women too. So I'm here to teach you a lesson, to see if you'll learn not to covet another woman's man. Like I said, I fell in love with Cosmo. When he went to my house

Deborah called me over to a corner and said, Andressa, he's the Laughing Assassin. He earns money for killing people. You, who're such a smarty pants, do you know why he got that name, Laughing Assassin? Because once, when he was starting out in his profession, he shot a guy, he thought the guy had died, and he took off. But the guy, who had taken three bullets, didn't die and later told the story that Cosmo, every time he took a shot, he laughed his ass off, and the story spread. So Cosmo became known as the Laughing Assassin. But this story that my cousin told me didn't scare me. Take a look at my house. It was built with our labor. If you didn't know this, now you do. I'm not only Cosmo's woman, I'm his partner. I realized that's what I wanted to do the first time Cosmo took me along to see him ice a guy. He earned more for a job that lasted fifteen minutes than I did in a whole month. And Cosmo enjoyed it. While I had to put up with the rich bitch screaming at me if I didn't iron her dress right. That day, when I saw Cosmo waste the guy and laughing every time he squeezed the trigger—three times like always—I tried to laugh but I couldn't. I started to tag along when he went out on jobs and one day he let me shoot some dumbass that had to be put away. And for the first time I laughed out loud. It's so good to kill someone who has to die. Because me and Cosmo just kill people who deserve it. But you don't deserve to die, that's why I'll spare you, you little cunt, I'll just put a mark on your face to warn other sluts who want to mess with my man. See how nice I am, I could take you out. You're still young, I hope you learn your lesson. See this blade? I'm going to cut both of your pink little cheeks. Stop screaming, you cow, or I'll cut your throat. So, that was quick, right? I'll wipe off the blood, disinfect it, cover it with gauze, and put on some tape. You should be crying, that's how people learn, by suffering. Now, get out, go to the hospital where the doctors can stitch you up. And if you go to the police, I'll kill you. Wait, I'll go out with you, I'll go look for Cosmo to see where he went to.

The Innocent

Luis Antônio is making me more and more nervous, and now he's taken to saying that I'm crazy. Me? Crazy! Just because in the last few months I've had some hallucinations? My nerves are rubbed raw, and he's to blame. He abandons me all day in this house I detest and when he arrives he doesn't really talk to me. I spend all afternoon in bed, I take some medicine to calm down, and I drink champagne. I love champagne. Last week I got a bit out of control. I saw the walls twisting and giant butterflies flitting around aimlessly. I was afraid they'd fall on my head. I tried to scream, but my voice wouldn't come out. Then I covered my entire body with the sheet. I calmed down, but I didn't have enough air, so I uncovered myself and the walls went on melting, I rubbed my eyes, pinched myself to make sure I was awake. It wasn't a dream and my panic grew. I tried to get out of bed, and my legs wouldn't obey me. I ordered them to move, beat them forcefully, they were alive because I could feel the pain from the blows. I threw myself to the floor, which seemed like quicksand, finally I managed to get up and, staggering, supported myself on the furniture to make it to the door. In the hallway, I cried and my breathing turned into panting. I leaned on the wall, letting all my weight rest against it. I was lucid, I remember Luis Antônio saying I'd gone crazy. But if I was tense he was to blame. He made me into this, this desperate person. My torment is the fruit of the hatred I feel for him. I may be crazy, but it's from rage. I thought about what to do, maybe aerobics, I mustn't put on weight. The most horrible thing in the world is fat people. I touched my body. I had nothing to worry about, I was thin. I can say I'm a pretty woman, not pretty, beautiful. There's not a single person who doesn't look at me when I go by. And in addition I'm chic and there's nothing stupid about me. Maybe that's been my downfall, being intelligent. I'm also rich, the problem is that my husband takes charge of my money. The cheat cut off my access, alleging that I'm not capable of managing either myself or my finances. He's to blame for my being like this, so tense. My heart starts racing suddenly all the time, it's a warning, I'm not going to be able to stand this torture much longer. Last week I had to have an electrocardiogram every day. I thought I'd feel better after the passing of my mother. How innocent I was, the witch died too late. As God is my witness, it wasn't for lack of praying. Speaking of that, I've decided to stop praying. Praying is something crazy people do. My mother wasn't worth anything, she was against me and in favor of that cripple Luis Antônio. It was unfair, two against one.

She detested me because I was prettier than her. I'll never forget, when I was little, I used to love smelling alcohol. The two of us were in the bathroom, she looked at herself in the mirror. Ugly people have the habit of looking at themselves in the mirror. I myself particularly detest mirrors, that's why last month I broke the mirror in my bathroom. I'm not superstitious, only crazy people believe that story about seven years' bad luck. Anyway, my mother had a bottle of ammonia in her hand. I thought it was alcohol and asked to smell it. She said, go ahead, it's alcohol. I inhaled deeply and began to cry. My nose burned. She started laughing and said it was to teach me to never again trust anyone. That may be the only good thing she ever taught me. But I didn't learn the lesson. And I trusted everyone. Can it be? Actually, I trust by mistrusting. That makes me suffer. And who should I trust? Luis Antônio? I'm not an idiot. I see everything. And when I tell him the truth, that I know he cheats on me, he says I'm crazy, that I'm obsessive, with too much time on my hands. He comes home with his shirt stained with lipstick and tells me to my face that I'm seeing things, there's no lipstick marks at all. I tell him to take off his shirt so I can show him the red stains. He implores me, Patricia, stop it. That angelic voice fills me with rage, the wretch speaks in that voice on purpose just to irritate me. Later he thinks I'm crazy because I ripped the shirt from his body. Luis Antônio is going to end up killing me from watching me so much. I have a driver who pursues me all day. The same one who takes me by force to the psychiatrist. All at Luis Antônio's command. My psychiatrist is cross-eyed, who ever heard of a cross-eyed psychiatrist? I don't want to create problems with my husband, so I take the pills the psychiatrist orders. I swear, during many of the sessions I feel like killing him in cold blood. Once, I tried to kill myself by taking two boxes of tranquilizers. I went into a coma but didn't die. That's true failure, not being competent enough to take your own life. The psychiatrist went to visit me in the hospital and I confessed that I wanted to die. He put on the expression of a thinking being and concluded that the act was a cry for help. I had an attack of hysteria, after all, I was paying and he didn't even know how to listen or make an intelligent comment. I wanted to die, or I would end up killing Luis Antônio, that miserly crippled fashion plate. When my mother finally died, I went shopping to celebrate, I paid a fortune for a dazzling dress to wear at the witch's funeral and Luis Antônio scolded me, said it wasn't proper for people to see me commemorating my mother's death. So he's the crazy one, not me. I have to admit, Luis Antônio is an excellent professional, but I pay a high price for being married to a successful lawyer, I have to go to every dinner, each one more boring than the last. And then he doesn't want me

to drink, and drinking is all that lets me stand it. He says I
get drunk and make a scene. He's been married to me for
years and still hasn't realized that I attract attention even
with my mouth shut. I'm a very pretty woman and still have
presence of mind. So it's natural that I attract attention. He
claims I say absurd things, just because a woman asked me
what I do, which between you and me is impolite, and I
replied that I beautify the world. And there's more, I adore
dancing and it's obvious that I arouse the attention of every
man at the party, even the married ones. What's the problem? I don't mind if they want to dance with Luis Antônio,
who's a very bad dancer. And if I only talk to men it's
because I have nothing in common with people of my own
sex. Luis Antônio says I like to stir up trouble, that I'm a flirt
and that's why I don't have any girlfriends. But he doesn't
know anything, the one who knew about things was my
favorite philosopher, Schopenhauer, who said that beautiful
and intelligent women are destined to live in isolation. And
that the others are blind with envy and rage at the superior
individual, me in this case. Luis Antônio wants to kill me.
What did I do to deserve a husband like that? I've tried
everything. Voodoo. Charms. I gave up, because that's
something crazy people do. If he still had sex with me, but
no, he only has sex with other women. He doesn't have sex
with me, doesn't give me money, doesn't praise me, and then

wants to tell me what to do. In another incarnation I want
to be born a lover. I'm getting nervous because Luis Antônio
hasn't arrived. Sometimes I think Luis Antônio doesn't have
sex with me just to punish me because I don't want to have
children. I don't. Having a child means starting to die, you
begin living to serve the next generation, another life that's
not your own. Besides, I detest children, they're like little
toads, they require a lot of attention, and I frankly don't
have time. I'm a very busy woman. And besides, that business of wanting children made me a bit jealous. All the time
telling me, let's have a child, I want a child, a child, a child,
a child . . . I came to hate that child even before it was con-
ceived. I'm a sensible person. Children are a problem, you
can't send them back even if they turn out to be defective,
they're for a lifetime. And killing a child is inadmissible,
something heartless people might do. Where is that man?
I'm going to have a sip of champagne before he gets here, I
don't want to listen to a sermon. It's impressive that I, a
dynamic and emancipated woman, married a man who's a
dictator. But I'm not afraid of him. It's eight o'clock, now
I've begun breaking into a cold sweat as the time approaches
for Luis Antônio to arrive. The champagne is evaporating,
it's gone in a minute. I'll open another bottle, but this time
I'll keep an eye on it. Oh, he's arrived, I'm going to hide the
bottle. See there, he doesn't even say hello, just a kiss on the

forehead. Who does he think he is? He's going straight to his office and turning on the computer. I suspect he masturbates watching pornography on the internet. That's why he doesn't screw me. But if he were a real man, that wouldn't be a problem. Luis Antônio doesn't approach me anymore, he has no desire to have sex with me. He claims he's tired. If I insist too much, he attacks me, saying he can't stand to look at me, drunk and doped up, wandering around the house. But I don't let it pass. Where does he get off calling me a drunk? Doped up? I hit him, I broke a plate over his head. I don't understand why he doesn't want to have sex with me. I'm pretty. Here he comes, dragging his foot. I think I must love the man because only a person who loves would be willing to go to bed with someone who drags one foot. I'm going to tear off my clothes, open my legs, and masturbate. He won't be able to resist. Luis, my love, come here. Luis, look at me, Luis, Luis, come be with me, Luis, I love you, make love to me, screw me, Luis, screw me if you're a man. Ah! You can't get it up, you piece of shit, talk to me, answer me. Luis Antônio stared at me in disgust, I began to think I was turning into some kind of insect. I screamed in fright, I thought I was growing wings. I screamed more and more, because I wanted him to come back to the living room. He didn't come. I insisted some more. I think I even cried. And the wretch didn't come to help me. He left me no alternative. I got up, went to the kitchen, opened the drawer where the knives are kept. So many knives. I stood there for a time, not knowing which one to choose. I picked out the biggest one. I went to the office. Luis Antônio had his back to me, playing solitaire on the computer. He did that on purpose. What was he trying to prove? That I mean less than that stupid little game? I had no doubts. I struck a single blow in his back. The fault was his. Now he's quiet and silent, fallen on the floor. Thank God. I'm going to have my champagne, without anyone bothering me.

The Ceiling

Marcos went into his bedroom and lay down on the bed without taking off his clothes. He looked at the ceiling, white and faded by time.

Turning his head to one side, he noticed one of the wardrobe doors ajar, allowing him to see his wife's clothes.

He looked at the ceiling again. He heard nothing, not even the restless beating of his heart. The silence caused a certain distress.

Panting, he couldn't breathe, feeling suffocated by his memories.

He looked at the ceiling, which was slowly lowering itself toward him. Marcos didn't move, not knowing how long he lay prostrate on the bed.

The ceiling continued to descend. His space was becoming constricted.

He stuck his face in the sheet, the pillowcase, and tried to take a deep breath. He wanted to sleep.

Waiting for the sleep that never came, he looked at the ceiling, which continued to come down, drawing ever closer to his head as if to pin him against the floor.

He noticed a flaw in the ceiling. He sat up in bed. From up close he could see a type of opening. A hole. Marcos stuck first the tip, then his entire finger into it. When he removed it, a piece of the ceiling came loose.

He stood on the bed and looked into the small hole. He saw nothing, just pitch black. He sat down on the bed again. He thought about the hole that opened onto darkness.

He got up and punched the ceiling, twice, and the hole enlarged. Using his hands, Marcos pulled away the edges of the hole. He stood on tiptoe and stuck his head through the opening he had made.

He saw the same thing as before. He kept his head there, and his vision gradually grew accustomed. After a time he made out something that seemed like fireflies in flight.

It was the sky.

He removed his head from the hole and went to get a mallet.

He stood on the bed and began striking the mallet against the ceiling.

With each blow, he watched pieces of plaster and cement fall.

The ceiling was totally destroyed and the entire sky came into his bedroom.

Marcos lay down on the rubble and stared.

Escaping Poverty

There's nothing worse than being middle class. You're nothing and, what's more, it takes daily effort to keep on being nothing.

To escape the impasse I decided to marry a rich man. But how to find him? I'd do it by going to rich people's clubs. Getting into those clubs was the easiest thing in the world if you went in the morning and were well dressed.

I got into the club by acting confident and waving to the security guard. I confess I didn't know where to go. I followed a guy who was carrying a tennis racket. The club had several courts, one of them was surrounded by bleachers and there I sat down. A fellow who was carrying a few kilos of excess weight sat next to me and asked, do you play tennis? I answered that I didn't. I don't either, but I should, I keep gaining weight, he said, snorting in snot from his nose. Since I specialized in flattering people, I answered, you're not overweight. He patted his belly and said, yes I am, and I eat too much. You should see how I eat; today you'll have lunch with me. He snorted again as if he had a sinus infection. I accepted the invitation.

We sat at a table near the pool. He called the waiter,

asked for vodka and orange juice for him and a flute of champagne for me. He didn't even ask me what I wanted to drink. As soon as they put a dish of nuts on the table, he scarfed them up and asked for more. You know who I am, don't you? I'm Dudu. I kept quiet. Son of Eduardo Xavier Bonarto.

I knew who his father was, I read the newspaper. I hit the jackpot, I thought, that guy was a super millionaire.

Dudu called over the waiter. Bring the baked fish for the young lady, a duck *à l'orange* for me, and some bread right away. He turned to me and asked my name. Mariana, I answered.

The bread arrived and he dived into the rolls, breadsticks, paté, and olives. He ordered a bottle of French red wine. You're very pretty, how old are you? Twenty-five. I'm twenty years older than you, I'm forty-eight. Do I look it? No, you look much younger, I answered. He bared his teeth and said, see, see? He tapped his knife lightly on his incisors. See? He opened his mouth wider as he snorted. I had all my teeth capped by Dr. Baltazar Lugano. Very nice, I said.

The food arrived and he asked, can I try your fish? And zap, he speared my fish with his fork, taking half of it, eating it in one bite. Before he even swallowed the fish, he took a bite of the duck. His way of eating would have repelled me, if he'd been someone else, but it was okay for him, he did it because he could, he was Dudu Xavier Bonarto. Then he ordered flan for both of us, with coffee and cookies. I hate flan, but that wasn't a problem because he ate his and mine.

When we finished, he said, my driver will take you home. It's a date, next weekend we'll go to my island on my yacht. I want my parents to meet you. Give my driver your number. He snorted.

When I got home, I ran in to tell my mother the news.

No joke, she exclaimed, Dudu Xavier Bonarto?

But I haven't told you everything yet, mom, he invited me to his *yacht,* to go to his *island*, and to meet his *parents*.

Sweetheart, this is your big chance!

The phone rang. It was Dudu. He was laconic. The driver will pick you up Saturday at eight a.m. to take you to the Yacht Club. From there we'll go to my island. Is it a date? Sure, I answered. So, I don't need to call again, we'll see each other the day after tomorrow, a kiss.

I couldn't sleep that night, imagining my wedding, how I should behave with his parents, the yacht, I had never been on a yacht, and the island, my God, it was too good to be true. Something told me that I'd marry him, it was fate. I imagined my life as a rich woman, trips, money to buy everything I have never had and always wanted.

The driver arrived at eight o'clock sharp. At the club, he

carried my bag as he led me to Dudu's yacht. He was waiting, wearing tennis whites, Bermudas, a knit shirt and a captain's cap. He posed at the helm, as if he were maneuvering the boat. This pantomime lasted only a short while. Then he said, to a man in a white uniform at his side, take the wheel, Mario.

We went to the aft deck and had a drink. I had champagne and he had his vodka and orange juice while we nibbled at snacks. I noted that he had a nervous tic, his right eye kept blinking, and his head had a light tremor. He talked about his yacht, his trips, and his apartments on Avenue Montaigne and Park Avenue. He also talked about the house on Capri, about millions of people I only knew by name.

Dudu's mother and father were waiting on the dock and they treated me very kindly.

Dudu introduced me as his girlfriend. He didn't kiss me when we were alone. When there were people present, he put his arm around me affectionately. He slept in the room next to mine, but didn't come to me during the night. I considered it a sign of respect. But I was intrigued.

I became Dudu's steady girlfriend; we saw each other every day. He put a car and driver at my disposal. Deep down, he wanted to control me, but I paid no attention, I loved having a car and driver.

Since Dudu had nothing to do, he demanded my company 24/7. I spent every weekend with him, on the island, or the country ranch, or in the penthouse where he lived. We slept in the same room, in the same bed, but he never touched me. He asked me to caress his head until he fell asleep. Once in a while we kissed, but that was on my initiative. I rubbed myself against him, but nothing seemed to excite him, so I gave up.

Dudu lived in a fantasy world. Every day was a day of recreation. Swim in daddy's pool, eat lunch out, talk on the phone, scold the thousand servants, talk on the phone again, go to parties and dinners. He couldn't sit still, appreciate anything, he said things that made no sense. His dysfunction was such that he couldn't even take a message. He couldn't write notes because he wasn't able to match the size of the handwriting to the size of the paper. He would ask me to take notes for him.

Dudu's friends loved to show up in the society pages. They would smile sincerely to the photographer but after the flash disappeared the magic was over. Dudu wanted me to laugh like them, he said, you don't know how to smile, go on, learn you can't come out in the pictures looking like someone at a funeral. I'll have to teach you how to smile.

I didn't like to admit it, but my boyfriend, in spite of his fortune, was not a generous person. He was lavish with himself but with others he was quite miserly. When we would go out in a group he never offered to pay the bill. That made me uncomfortable.

By this time he had become intimate with me, and this intimacy was increasingly more disagreeable. I had to watch him get dressed and tell him he was handsome, that he hadn't gained weight, anything he did I had to look at. He demanded excessive attention. If we were on the island, I was forced to watch him swim, to observe a bald man with a big head swim and wave like a five-year-old child asking for his mother's attention. He insisted on detailing his intestinal disturbances, if he had gone to the bathroom, how many times, hard or soft, if he had needed a glycerin suppository.

One morning the driver picked me up at home. Instead of taking me to the club, he said that Dr. Eduardo Xavier Bonarto was waiting for me in his office.

The old man received me saying, Mariana, I decided to invite you here because I've made a decision: you and Dudu will get married. He has to change the life he's been leading, he'll be forty-nine years old, and I can't permit him to continue with his vices and extravagances. He must marry, have a family and children.

Rich people only like to marry rich people. But Dudu's case was so desperate that his family wanted him to marry,

even if it was with a middle-class girl like me. The old man
called his secretary on the intercom and asked her to call
his son. Dudu arrived, listened to his father in silence.
Obediently, after being given a box with a diamond ring in
it, he put the ring on my finger and asked me to marry him.

My family was invited to lunch at the Xavier Bonato res-
idence. They were very friendly and lunch went on in a cor-
dial atmosphere. Old Eduardo, as if asking for the approval
of my parents, announced that the engaged couple would
take a trip and that they would marry when they returned,
his wife would take care of all preparations for the religious
ceremony, including the reception. My father didn't like the
idea of us traveling together before we got married, but said
nothing.

We went straight to the VIP lounge at the airport. The
check-in and baggage check were handled by an employee
in my future father-in-law's company. I followed Dudu, who
walked quickly ahead of me. We sat in the VIP lounge,
where we got our boarding passes. He hardly looked at me,
he drank one glass of vodka after the other, but nothing
bothered me, I felt good in those surroundings. I looked at
my reflection in a mirror, I was a beautiful woman with a
flute of champagne in my hand and a Chanel bag on my lap.
I was in love with myself.

Settled in my first-class seat, all of Dudu's defects seemed insignificant. I reminded myself that I was there because of him. I wanted to kiss him. Dudu refused my kiss. I asked for champagne. He drank what was probably his tenth vodka.

The plane landed. We collected our baggage and went to a waiting car. Paris, Paris, I repeated to myself. Everything was beautiful, the people, the trees, the gardens, the buildings, the cafés, there couldn't be a lovelier city on earth.

The apartment on Avenue Montaigne was a duplex, with high ceilings and enormous windows through which light streamed that accentuated the richness of the furniture. On the first floor were the social rooms, kitchen, and servants' quarters. A marble staircase led to the upper floor where there were bedrooms, a sitting room, and several other spaces. I stayed in one suite and he in another.

We had lunch and then each of us went to our own room. I took a bath, unpacked my things, and went down to the living room. I stood at the window, watching people walk by. Dudu didn't leave his room; I was getting impatient, crazy to go out and walk the streets of Paris, to see the city. I couldn't wait any longer and went to his room. I knocked on the door. He didn't answer. I knocked again and said, let's go for a walk. He answered without opening the door, not today, tomorrow you can go for a walk.

I spent the rest of the day looking out the window. It

got dark and I stayed there, looking out at the street and thinking.

Mariana, Dudu shouted, Mariana, get dressed. I took a bath, got dressed and waited for him in the living room. Since Dudu didn't come down I went to his room. I knocked on the door and went in. He was sitting in an armchair in front of a table, where there were several lines of coke. I said, I'm waiting for you in the living room.

We went to a party, in an enormous apartment, where we stayed about a half hour. That was the time it took for Dudu to drink and eat everything in front of him. When his hunger was sated, we went to a bar. Then we went on to some nightclubs, other parties, other bars, more nightclubs. I lost count of how many places we went to and the number of people Dudu knew. I noticed he looked at beautiful men and women with equal interest. We got home at daybreak. We had breakfast and went to sleep. I slept all day.

When I got up, I found Dudu sitting on the living room sofa crying. He asked me to hug him. Feeling my arms around him he cried harder, like a child. I had never seen anyone look so sad, but I felt no pity.

We stayed in Paris for a week. I didn't see the Louvre, or the Orsay Museum or any other museum, not even the Eiffel Tower. All we did was go to restaurants and nightclubs, and I walked the streets near Dudu's apartment, where the best stores were located. Dudu gave me two dresses. For himself, he bought an infinite number of things—pants, shirts, jackets, shoes, luggage, socks, shorts, scarves, handkerchiefs, gloves, and a hat he would certainly never wear.

We went to the airport, but a little before we were going to check in Dudu said, we're not going to Rome, I hate Italy and the Italians. He waved his hands as if in caricature and talked in what he imagined to be an Italian accent: *Mamma mia, porca miseria, cazo in culo, prego, capisce.*

We returned to the apartment on Avenue Montaigne. My week in Paris lasted a month. And what did I do during that time?

Every other day, Dudu yelled from the bathroom, Mariana, Mariana, bring my glycerin suppository, quick. I would get the suppository from his room, go to the bathroom where he was sitting on the toilet, kneel by his side and stick the suppository up his anus. His penis would start to get hard. He ordered, deeper, Mariana, stick your finger in deeper, that's why I cut your nails. I would do as he asked. Dudu then would start to masturbate, while he said, Mariana, suck my cock. But that I did not do as he asked. His hand movements would become more rapid and he'd come, trying to ejaculate in my face. Normally I was hit in the throat and on my shoulder. I'd run out to my bathroom where I'd take a long shower, soaping myself down repeatedly.

During the rest of the day I'd have the impression that a nauseating smell emanated from my finger. It didn't matter how many times I washed my hands. Those days, I always lost my appetite. No matter how good the restaurant was, I couldn't eat. Eat up, Dudu would say, grinding his teeth, I'm paying a fortune for this entrée. While he admonished me, he stabbed at my plate with his fork until he emptied it. Then he reprimanded me, I'm gaining weight because you don't eat.

There was another disagreeable ritual, cutting Dudu's nails on his right hand and his toenails. He cut the nails of his left hand with his innumerable scissors. He insisted that I cut the nails of his right hand the exact length of those on his left. He refused to get manicures and pedicures, saying that all the nail techs had AIDS. This routine lasted for hours. In between hand and foot and then between one foot and the other he took a break to snort cocaine. One day he'd snorted too much and, not liking how I cut the nails of his left foot, he kicked me in the chest. I told him to go to hell and went to my room. Hours later, he knocked on my door with an enormous package from Hermes. It was a Kelly Bag. I had always wanted one of those bags. But the happiness it gave me was of short duration since a little later he called me to trim his nose hairs with a little electric device. His nose hairs were abundant and grew out daily.

Every night we watched movies in a media room. We watched porn movies. I liked watching, I would get excited. Once Dudu asked me to take off my clothes and to masturbate while he watched. He sat on the floor while I, reclined in an armchair with my legs spread, masturbated as I watched the film. I came. Dudu, after watching me for a while, started to masturbate, still sitting on the floor. Suddenly he got up and ejaculated on my face. His ejaculate seemed to stick on my nose and mouth. I tasted the toilet water taste of that viscous semen.

Dudu left the apartment right after lunch the next day. A little later he came back with a young man and said, today you are going to masturbate me while he butt-fucks me.

I couldn't take it any longer. I went to my room where I locked myself in. Later Dudu knocked on the door, with the altered voice of someone high on drugs. He said, you can come out, the fag left; I'm going to take a nap.

I opened up all the doors of my closet and picked up the Kelly Bag, with its soft leather, its perfect metal clasp, what refined finishing. Inside the bag that magic word: Hermes. I put the bag on the bed.

I crammed my clothes into the new Vuitton. I went to Dudu's room, he was asleep. I took one of his credit cards and some money from his wallet. In the dark my diamond engagement ring suddenly sparkled. I deserved that jewel.

I called the airlines and bought a coach class ticket to Brazil using Dudu's credit card. I was lucky; there was a seat on the flight to São Paulo that night. I left the credit card on a table. I had two hours to get to the airport.

After I checked in, I was suddenly hungry again. Luckily I had just enough cash to buy a cheeseburger with large fries and a Coke that I devoured with great pleasure before boarding the plane.

Bianca and Me

It was hard to please a woman like Bianca, who when she awoke in the morning, didn't have bad breath and a wrinkly face. When she woke up she didn't move and sometimes didn't even open her eyes. It was as if there were no difference between waking and sleeping, breathing and not breathing. Her apathy in relation to the world was great, even to her own life. Nothing seemed to interest her; she spoke in an indifferent, cold tone of voice, with a disdainful inflection as if she had a low opinion of everyone, even me, who she claimed to love. She yawned when she made love, coughed in disgust when she smoked, and chewed without pleasure when eating even the most delicious dish when we dined together.

At times I had the impression that for Bianca, being with me or not didn't alter her existence, while I only had to think about not having her at my side to die a little. When I talked to her about my wish to introduce her to my family she didn't look at me, and smiled as if she hadn't heard what I said. She was a strange person, she'd drink vodka straight and not get drunk. When she was sober and in a bad mood, she'd walk with a stagger, with slow movements like a drunk. She would throw herself on the couch as if exhausted.

Once a week, Bianca would bring Gustavo home. She'd dress up in a seductive outfit, wearing a dress and heels to receive him, because that's what he liked. She wanted to please him in any way she could, and when I pointed this out to her, she denied it vehemently, alleging that she also got dressed up that way for me. It was true, in a way. She asked me to clean up the house and prepare Gustavo's favorite cocktails. Sometimes I was the one who would go shopping. Because of me, Bianca rarely would go out to dinner or sleep somewhere else with him. After I moved in with her, Bianca never traveled again with Gustavo, so I wouldn't get upset.

As soon as the doorbell rang, I'd go to my room, taking my dinner with me on a tray, and then I'd lock the door. In the room, I'd brood jealously and would lose my appetite and couldn't sleep, I chain-smoked, paced, and tried to hear what was going on in the living room.

I never laid eyes on Gustavo. I just saw his photo, after much insisting. In the only photo I saw, Bianca looked like a dwarf next to him, he must have been almost six feet tall.

I never talked bad about Gustavo or made offhand remarks about him because I knew that sooner or later

Bianca would get tired of his company. Behind the door I tried to hear what went on in the living room, but I couldn't. Bianca told me that Gustavo wanted to take her to the bedroom, the only one in the house. But she explained it was being renovated.

With no other alternative, Gustavo would take her on the red couch or on the rug in the living room. I never heard a sound from her; she must have been yawning in her indifferent way. Bianca preferred to have sex passively. She liked to remain immobile receiving pleasure. She came in silence or she faked it, deceiving Gustavo, or at least that's what she said. With me she came with a small sigh.

The only thing Bianca complained about was the way he sometimes talked to her, as if she were a complete imbecile. I'm sure that Bianca must have thought he was the imbecile. Gustavo was vain and he didn't notice she dismissed him, or so she told me. Gustavo is an object, she repeated, when she was in bed with me, you're the one I love.

When Gustavo left, I filled the bathtub with warm water and went to get her. Normally Bianca would be lying naked on the red couch waiting for me. One night, before we took a bath, I lay down next to her and when I caressed her, I noticed her vagina was wet. The odor that emanated from her was the same as when she had sex with me. I asked if, contrary to what she told me, she reached orgasm with

Gustavo. Bianca laughed and walked to the bathroom. I followed. When I walked into the bathroom she was already in the tub. I decided not to bring it up again. I washed her hair and kissed her tenderly.

After the bath, as was our custom, I poured vodka for us. She laughed when she told me random stories that in some way, at least in her head, made sense. Maybe it was to hide her nervousness. I chain-smoked. I couldn't repress her.

Some days later, I invited Bianca for a weekend out of town. She loved those excursions. What she didn't know was that I had hired a technician to install a camera in the bookshelf so I could record what happened in the living room. The images would be transmitted to a small monitor that I would hide in my things.

I never stopped studying and working, which according to Bianca, was crazy; after all, she had enough money to take care of me. She received an allowance from a trust fund from her father and said it was the most wonderful thing that could happen to anyone. Her parents had died in an accident when she was a little girl.

Bianca and I met at the College of Fine Arts. I graduated and she dropped out in the first year, claiming she knew more than the ignorant professors.

I remember the first day I saw her. I thought she was strange, dressed all in black, her eyes heavily made up in black and hair dyed black. She smoked with a cigarette holder.

One day I was in a state of acute depression but even so I went to classes. However, in the middle of a painting class, a physical pain overcame me. I left the room and sat in the stairwell. Bianca approached and observed me. Standing, she offered me a cigarette.

It was forbidden to smoke in the building, but she appeared not to know this. I refused, but asked her to sit next to me.

I explained that there was no reason for my suffering. After smoking three cigarettes, Bianca left. A few minutes later she returned with my books, pulled me by the arm, and said, come with me.

I followed Bianca, talking without a pause. We walked for more than an hour. Finally we got to a park where I thought we would sit down. But I was wrong; she didn't stop, didn't look in my direction, and remained silent as if not hearing a word I was saying. Since I didn't stop complaining, Bianca slapped me. I didn't react. She slapped me again, harder. I reacted angrily, shaking her by the shoulders. We ended up on the grass. Bianca started to laugh and so did I. She offered me a cigarette, this time I accepted. We smoked and looked at the sky.

Bianca rolled over on to me and kissed me. Her skin was

soft. It was a quick kiss. I wanted to kiss her again.

We went to her house, which was next to the park.

It was an old building with one apartment on each floor. When Bianca opened the door, the light from the enormous windows blurred my vision.

The apartment was large, with high ceilings, wood floors with marble sections, and in the middle of the room was a red velvet couch. One of the walls of the living room had a wall-to-wall bookshelf. Only later did I learn that Bianca hadn't read any of the books, they'd been bought by the yard as decoration. The only comfortable space in the house aside from the kitchen and two bathrooms was Bianca's room, which had red walls and a black ceiling. Dangling from a crystal chandelier was a little devil. She said it was made of cloth and it was for good luck.

Then night fell and in the dark objects turned whiter, just like Bianca's body. Her breasts were small, her iliac bones seemed to pierce her skin, and I could see her ribs. I traversed them with my fingertips and tongue. I had never experienced such strong and lasting pleasure. I had discovered a new life with this woman. That's when she told me about Gustavo, her boyfriend, but she added quickly that now that she'd met me she didn't want anything more to do with him. But she needed some time to end the relationship.

In the beginning I went along with her plan to keep

seeing Gustavo, but she never stopped seeing him. That's why I decided to install a camera, since I couldn't identify exactly the sounds I heard in the living room.

I was surprised when I saw the first images on the monitor. Gustavo only became erect after Bianca stroked him and sucked him. Contrary to what she said, it was she who provoked him to have sex. Only after Gustavo was turned on did she assume a passive position, as she did with me. When I saw on the screen that he was penetrating her, I wanted to open the door and beat him up. But I controlled myself and waited for Gustavo to leave before confronting her.

Then I gave her an ultimatum: Gustavo or me. In that moment, Bianca approached me, embraced me, and said, please don't leave. I've never liked Gustavo or anyone else. I love you.

I could not resist her kisses and we went to bed. I licked her body eagerly and for the first time Bianca performed cunnilingus on me. Afterward, lying side by side, Bianca said, Marta, I love you.

On second thought, I won't ever leave her. If she wants to be with some man, she can go ahead; I know it's just a passing diversion. But another woman? No, I'll kill her if she does that.

A Happy Marriage

I got to the club in the morning. Ricardo was sitting on the veranda, reading, with his legs sticking out from under the table. Now or never, I thought. I went to the bar, bought a bottle of water, filled a glass almost to overflowing, and walked toward him. I tripped over his legs and spilled water on them.

I apologized. Ricardo replied that it was no problem and went back to reading the book he was holding. "My name is Laura," I said. He made a vague gesture, nodded his head, and continued to read.

I'd been trying to talk to Ricardo for some time but never had the courage to interrupt his reading. But that day I decided to go all the way.

"What's the book you were reading?"

He answered that it was a book on financial mathematics.

I stood there not knowing what to say. Ricardo noticed and asked impatiently if I needed anything.

I said the first thing that came into my head, that I was unsure whether to go to college or be a housewife, which is what I'd really like to be.

Ricardo looked at me and replied, "Then be a housewife."

"Being a housewife isn't easy. I need a husband, but the person I like doesn't like me. Actually, he doesn't even know I like him."

"Tell him: I like you. Problem solved."

"I like you."

Ricardo looked at me and said, pensively, "Housewife, huh?"

That's how it began. We went to the movies, went out to dinner, he met my family and I met his.

Sundays he liked to have lunch at my house. Those days the maid was off, so all the work was done by my mother and me. After lunch, Ricardo would go to the living room and smoke cigars with my father, while my mother and I cleared the table, washed the dishes, and made them coffee.

When I served the coffee, Ricardo kissed my cheek and said, "I enjoyed hearing you and your mother laughing and talking while doing the dishes."

Before long, Ricardo asked me to marry him. While Mom and I dried our tears, my father, in a solemn tone, said he was honored to give his daughter's hand, and added that he, Ricardo, was marrying a serious, responsible, and obedient young woman.

We rented a nice apartment near my parents' home. I insisted on arranging it according to Ricardo's taste. I always made his favorite dishes for dinner. He was often late, but

I waited. Sometimes Ricardo would arrive very late, saying he'd already had a sandwich at the office. That bothered me a little. I would end up having dinner by myself because as soon as Ricardo arrived he would sit down in front of the computer and work until late. Many nights I would go to sleep before him and not even notice when he came into the bedroom. In the morning we'd have a quick chat. He was always in a hurry.

My days came to be very long. Ricardo barely spoke to me. I had to find something to do, and nothing seemed better than to have a child. I stopped taking the pill but didn't say anything to my husband, who only wanted to have children after he made head of the department where he worked.

When I very nervously told Ricardo that I was pregnant, I explained immediately that I hadn't gone off the pill and didn't know how it happened. I saw he wasn't happy with the news; his only reaction was a resigned sigh. He didn't have the courage to suggest that his sweet little bourgeois wife get an abortion. But he remained in a bad mood for a long time. When the test results indicated that the child's sex was male, he smiled for the first time in months.

The child was born and I decided he would have the name of Ricardo's father, which made my husband happy. It wasn't exactly a name that appealed to me, but . . .

At my son's first birthday party, my mother asked me if I was happy. I thought before answering and said, "I really love my son but can't say I'm happy. I'm even thinking of having another child. At times Ricardo seems not to see me and isn't even aware that I exist."

My mother smiled and answered: "Your father's like that too. He doesn't hear a thing I say. But don't worry, those are the marriages that last a lifetime."

Piglet and Mouse

It was love at first sight. After all, is there anything more beautiful in the world than a blond, plump, blue-eyed woman with pink skin, big thighs, and a luscious behind that makes you want to bite it? Is there? No, and Cristiane, my girlfriend, was just like that. Still, I'd decided to end our relationship. We had been together a while. I never doubted that I loved her, but she bored me, and she was starting to get on my nerves. She was prim and proper, had good common sense, and she tried to take care of me. She wanted to get married and have children, like every woman.

I called Cristiane from work to tell her that I'd pick her up at eight o'clock, as we'd agreed.

I went home to change, but there was no time, so I decided to smoke a joint to calm down. The next thing I knew, it was quarter to eight. I couldn't delay. Cristiane was punctual and considered it disrespectful if I didn't arrive at the appointed time.

While I was driving to pick her up I started to think. I was already losing patience with myself, it wasn't the first time that I had planned to end the relationship and couldn't do it.

I honked but Cristiane was already waiting for me at the

door to her building. She was incapable of making me wait. She walked, almost skipped, to the car; the way she walked was charming. Since I'm a gentleman, I got out of the car and opened the door for her. I kissed her and said, "Hello, Piglet."

Before I continue, I should explain something. As soon as we started to go out, I gave Cristiane the affectionate name of piglet—as I said before she was pink and round like a new suckling pig. During the course of the relationship I started to call her piglet, my pigsley, and things like that. She didn't mind, she knew it was meant affectionately. Since I'm a short, small guy, Cristiane called me mouse, and I liked that too.

"Mouse," she said before she got into the car, "what are you wearing? Are you still in your work clothes? I can't believe you went to work in those shoes. Didn't I tell you to throw them out?"

Cristiane was always bossing me around and I obeyed her, without complaint. While I drove, Cristiane observed me with an inquisitive look that was at the same time a look of love. That exasperated me, I would have to summon up my courage and end it with her. I answered no, without looking at her. When we stopped at a light, Cristiane turned on the dashboard light and grasped my chin, turning my face in her direction.

"Mouse, tell the truth. Did you smoke pot again?"

I said nothing and turned off the light. I accelerated. She wagged her head and said, "How many times do I have to ask you to stop that? Smoking marijuana is illegal, I don't think it can damage your health and I'm not really against it, but it's not legal. I don't like you to do anything that's against the law. Not to mention that people like you feed the drug trade. Please, my love, promise me that was the last time."

"I promise." I don't know why I answered that way, but my plan of ending the relationship was starting badly.

In the restaurant I didn't have to pull out Cristiane's chair because the waiter did it for me. We sat facing each other. Once again she looked at me with that in-love look that demands recognition, reciprocation, smiles, kisses, and sweet nothings. I didn't respond because I was afraid of giving in to her and once again giving up on ending it.

I called the waiter. Cristiane wanted a *caipirinha*. I decided to have one too. She ordered pasta to start and a veal *milanesa* as a main dish. When I asked for a salad she interrupted me. "Salad? Absolutely not, that's not people food. I chose an Italian restaurant so you would eat pasta. Order a *gnocchi al pesto*, you like it, and then have a meat dish. You need protein, you're too skinny."

I didn't argue and thought, Cristiane is becoming a real

pain in the ass. She's always telling me what to do, imagine if I married her.

"My love," said Cristiane, "choose a wine."

"I'm not going to drink wine today, but get some for yourself."

"What do you mean, mouse? Have some with me."

"I don't want any."

"Then choose a glass for me."

I decided to have wine and ordered a bottle.

She drank the wine looking at me amorously. I avoided eye contact. I felt an urgent need to tell her what I was planning. I breathed deeply, ready to finally speak. All I could manage to say was: "You're beautiful." She really was very pretty, wearing a tight blouse that accentuated her shape, showing her cleavage.

"Thanks, mouse, but tell me. What's going on? We women have a sixth sense; I know something's going on with you."

At that moment the waiter served the first dishes. Cristiane looked at her dish and began to eat. I enjoyed watching her taste the food with so much enthusiasm.

"It's delicious," she said, "aren't you going to eat?"

"No, I'm not hungry."

I started to sweat.

"I love you," she said.

She must have known what I was planning, that's why she said it. I dripped sweat, not saying a word.

"Mouse, do you like me?"

"I do."

"So why don't you say so? I always have to ask you. You never tell me spontaneously that you love me."

"You don't have to say those things, you just feel it."

I started to sweat more profusely. What was I saying? I looked at Cristiane, who was chewing her food. She lifted the fork slowly, opened her mouth, and stuck the food into it ever more slowly. I still hadn't touched my food. I wanted to leave, but Cristiane didn't stop eating. She'll never finish, I'll die here. I was getting desperate. How would I get rid of her?

"My love," said Cristiane, "what are you thinking about? Why aren't you eating? Don't you feel well?"

"Cristiane, I need to talk to you."

Since I wasn't able to say a word, I gave up on broaching the subject and, as always, started to relax and enjoy her company. When I noticed what had happened to me, I got upset. I paid the bill and, in a bad mood, dropped her off at her house. We said good-bye with a kiss. I watched her walk into the building and once again realized that I was a wimp.

When I got to my apartment, the first thing I did was phone Cristiane to let her know I was home safe and sound.

I was on edge after messing up again, and on that night I decided to leave her a message on her cell phone, ending it once and for all. She turned off her phone when she went to bed. Just to be safe, I waited until four in the morning before I called.

"Piglet," I said after the beep, "my pigsley, you know I love you, that you are very special to me, but I've been thinking a lot about us in the last few months . . . I wanted to speak to you in person but my nerve failed me. I couldn't, I tried and—" At that point a recording came on saying my time was up. Shit, I can't even do this by phone. I called again.

"Cristiane, what I want to say is, it's over, you suffocate me and I need time."

I hung up and went to bed.

The next day she didn't call me, nor did she call over the weekend. On Saturday I went to the movies, I stood in a long line to see a bad film. I always tell myself that when the film is bad, I'll leave in the middle, but I never do, I watch the crappy movie to the end.

On Monday I went to work. The day had barely started when Helen, my secretary, told me there was a man at the reception desk with a package for me. I asked her to let him in. Helen opened the door to my office. A corpulent man appeared, dressed in a kind of white, grimy jacket. He was holding an enormous cardboard box that jiggled on its own in his hands.

He gave me a red envelope. I recognized Cristiane's handwriting immediately. It said "For you, mouse."

I know this story might seem implausible and even absurd but it's the unvarnished truth.

When I took the box that was shaking on its own in the man's strong arms, something jumped to the floor. Helen started to scream. It was a piglet with red ribbons around its neck. The hellish beast was running around in circles in my office.

Helen called security to get the pig, which was knocking over chairs, ramming against the desk and the conference table. She ran after the animal to catch it but it kept escaping. When security arrived, they tried to pen it in, but the pig scooted through Helen's legs and ran out of my office. It ran along the hall, and other office workers tried to grab it. It was chaos, women screaming, men running after the pig that like a bat out of hell was knocking over everything in its path.

I wasn't able to catch it. I stood there thinking. I was fascinated by that little pink piglet that Cristiane had sent me. It was a real gesture of love. Cristiane would become my wife, I decided at that moment. She was the right woman to become the mother of my children.

The pig was finally caught by security. It was female. I put it in my arms, caressed it. Its skin was silky like Cristiane's. I walked into my office that like everything else on the floor was a mess. I sat with the piglet on my lap. As I stroked it, I made up my mind to call Cristiane.

She accepted my proposal of marriage.

Youth

I was once young but didn't know it. When I reached twenty-five I decided I didn't want to get any older. I couldn't stand the thought of turning into an old woman.

I remember when I first became aware of the tragedy. Walking down the street, I saw a woman in the distance. She was beautiful, had golden skin, a slim body, long blond hair. I was happy that she was coming toward me. Harmonious proportions, perfection of form, whether in a man or a woman, have always attracted me. I wanted to take a look at her, but when she passed by me I had a horrible surprise. She looked like an aged child. A kind of dead fetus. Her blue eyes were faded, with deep wrinkles around them, her hair was so sparse that I could see her scalp, and her skin was creased by the sun and especially by time. I felt afraid and thought, People with dignity shouldn't live past thirty-five.

I recall that I pinched my skin that day to make sure I was alive. Alive and twenty-five, I pondered and came to the conclusion that I had five more years ahead of me, ten at most. I wouldn't make it past thirty-five. They say a person can be beautiful, even youthful at fifty. But that's a lie; no one is young after thirty-five. In a few years I'd blow my brains out, I thought, getting old is creepy, you can't look at yourself in the mirror anymore. I imagined a bulging belly, varicose veins, wrinkles, cellulite on the thighs, and even if I stayed thin, my skin would droop, my body would be covered with folds of skin.

I went on looking at people in the street, all of them, without exception, horrible, misshapen, old, bent, badly dressed. I would walk through the most upscale area of the neighborhood and everything seemed repugnant. Despair enveloped me; every minute I spent looking at those people was one more fragment of my youth lost.

I've always been a practical person, and I calculated that if I didn't plan to kill myself before thirty-five, I would have to take care of my body. I couldn't continue going to sleep every night after four a.m., and I'd have to stop drinking, smoking, and eating chocolate mousse.

Life is shit, I thought when I saw an old man pass by. I'll never forget the sound of his bones cracking when he approached me. His steps were slow; if he fell he'd have a hard time getting up. I asked myself: What would I do? Help him up or step on him? It was obscene for him to go on living.

Nervous, I went into a bar and sat at a small table by the

sidewalk. I ordered a strong drink, smoked a few cigarettes, ordered a large serving of pudding with lots of syrup. I knew I was doing everything wrong and contributing to my premature ageing. But life wasn't so terrible that way. True, I looked at the people and they were still ugly. But now I was laughing at it all, at the grotesque world. I opened my makeup kit and touched up my lipstick. Wonderful, night was falling and I looked even prettier. Under that light, not a wrinkle was visible. I wasn't the witch I viewed with fright under the noonday sun. I could live till thirty-five at night and at noon promptly commit suicide.

I ordered another drink. My cell phone rang, but I didn't answer. It was my boyfriend. I paid the bill and started walking home. There weren't as many monstrous people loose on the street, or at least I don't remember seeing them.

As soon as I got home, the first thing I did was closely examine a photo taken when I was eighteen. I, a woman of twenty-five on her way to becoming a ruin, thought, That piece of paper was all that was left of my youth. I tore up the photo; it was proof that I had gotten old.

I went to the window. The telephone rang again. It was my boyfriend. I answered. I knew that the solution to my anxiety was sex, which always made me forget, even if fleetingly, what depressed me the most: physical decline. Sadly, it wasn't enough to avoid the curse of getting old someday. But at least I felt younger, more alive. I told him to come over. I remember I thought, Sex without commitment would be better, but I was already too old for that. Twenty-five is old.

The doorbell rang. It was him, my boyfriend. The door was open and I shouted, Come in.

From the living room I carefully observed my boyfriend and the view from my apartment. I lived on the twentieth floor, perfect for a fatal leap. But I preferred sex, which dissipated my somber thoughts.

Before giving myself to him, I always thought, Make love or jump out the window?

The doubt persists.

Today I'm married to my boyfriend. I'm forty-five and have two children.

I continue looking at myself in the mirror and going to the window to measure the height of the fall.

The Story of João and Maria

The only one who knows the story I am about to tell, besides me, is Maria.

My name is João.

I met Maria at the house of a mutual acquaintance and we fell in love. Maria decided we should live together. The truth is I was the one who benefitted from the arrangement. She put my life in order. I'm an interior decorator, I have a huge clientele. The problem was that half of my clients didn't pay me and I didn't know how to collect what they owed me. Maria took care of this; I never imagined I could earn so much money. She also put an end to my spendthrift ways. I only bought what she authorized me to purchase. I wasn't capable of learning how to drive, I would get too nervous. One of the first things Maria did was to fire the chauffeur and trade in my imported car for a more economical, Brazilian-made vehicle. I never would have thought that a woman could drive so well. Maria stopped working and started to administer my affairs. She was able to pay off a bank loan I had without having to ask my mother for help. She organized dinners and parties at our house without the assistance of the numerous people I was accustomed to paying to cater these affairs. My economic, social, and emotional life improved fantastically. Maria was a blessing from heaven.

My mother liked Maria and always asked me when we would give her a grandchild. It was a delicate situation. To head her off from bringing up the subject every time she talked with me, I used the first excuse that came into my head: that Maria was barren. I added that she was doing a treatment at a fertility clinic; we hadn't lost hope yet. Wouldn't you know that my mother called up Maria and told her she had made a promise to Our Lady of Miracles that she would give a special offering if her treatment was successful. Maria, who was very smart, thanked her without knowing what she was talking about. When we met later, Maria said, holy shit, João, what crap were you telling your mother?

I should open up a parenthesis here to explain that Maria had a very dirty mouth, but she used bad language without the slightest bit of aggression. At first this bothered me, because I didn't like to hear curse words. For that reason, when she challenged me, before I explained why I lied, I gave her a little kiss. She said, it was a good idea, but next time warn me. And she told me that she'd finally received the call she'd been waiting for and that she had made an appointment for the next day.

On the spot, I proposed that we go to a store where I'd seen a very pretty red, low-cut dress that would fit her body like a glove. I wanted to give her something new to bring her good luck at the appointment. I'm superstitious. She tried it on, but before authorizing me to buy the dress she wanted to know the price.

As was my custom, I helped Maria get dressed, choosing her shoes, her handbag, and accessories. After she left I organized the bathroom, because she was a bit of a slob. She left towels on the floor, makeup scattered on the sink counter, toothpaste tube open, panties hanging from the shower head. Then I had dinner and settled down to read. It wasn't yet midnight when Maria came home. I asked how her meeting had gone and she answered that it had been proof of the saying that appearances can be deceiving. Then she added that she couldn't understand how a man like Lucio, who was tall, elegant, and handsome, could be so gross. She was right, Lucio was a brute.

As soon as Maria arrived at the guy's apartment, he grabbed her, put his hand on her breast, pushed her to the bedroom, and threw her on the bed. I didn't worry because Maria told me she made him wear a condom. Then he served himself a glass of scotch and offered one to her, but she asked for champagne. All he had, if you can imagine it, is whiskey and beer. These men don't understand a thing about women.

Don't they get it that a woman with any self-respect loves champagne? But that wasn't all. I went crazy with hate when Maria got to the end of the story. The jerk had the nerve to turn on the television and say he couldn't miss a show that he liked, and she could leave if she wanted. Of course, Maria came right home.

I made her a sandwich and consoled her until she fell asleep. The next day, when I woke her up so we could play golf, she was already feeling a little better.

On the golf course the caddie, a muscular young man with a pleasant appearance, was already waiting for us. I noticed that he was looking at Maria with undisguised lust. But we had a rule: we didn't get involved with people of lower social and cultural standing. So, however attractive the caddie might be, the only thing he could do with Maria was look at her with a desire that would never be satisfied.

Since Maria and I didn't have the same handicap, I went on playing with Anselmo, even though we didn't get along. That day he outdid himself. Not content with telling me I'd gained a few pounds recently, every time he got a chance he'd say, hey fatty, it's your turn, and, listen tubby, you aren't playing so well. I told Maria and she said that Anselmo was jealous and was taking advantage of my neurosis about gaining weight, my obsession with losing weight, just to irritate me. Then she said I should ignore Anselmo and expand my circle of friends, forget him. I decided to go out that night to a new bar that had just opened. I invited Maria to go, but she preferred not to accompany me.

The bar was full. It was more a nightclub than a bar, and the music was very loud. I sat at the bar, ordered a scotch, and watched the people. Nobody interested me. I walked around and then I saw someone on the dance floor who caught my eye. I approached, and moving to the rhythm of the music, I said, you dance very well. It wasn't long before we were kissing.

Maria was startled when she saw me coming into the house. My face was still bleeding a little and I could hardly open my right eye. After cleaning me up and applying some medicine to my wounds, she sat on the living room sofa and I laid my head on her lap. I felt better because I was at home with my wife, and I calmly told Maria what had happened.

After kissing the guy I'd met at the bar, he invited me to his apartment. I accepted the invitation. He was a gorgeous man—he was tall, buff, and young. It was impossible to resist him, I explained to Maria, who listened attentively. When we got to the guy's house, he took off his clothes and ordered me to take off mine. As soon as I was naked, he kneeled in front of me and began to fellate me, but for some reason I couldn't reach orgasm. The guy said, I give up, it's your turn. I did as he asked. Afterward we kissed for a while and I felt some pleasure. Suddenly he interrupted the kiss and asked me to sodomize him. But looking at him kneeling on the sofa, exhibiting his buttocks and his hairy back—he looked like a monkey—my erection wilted. Then I said, I'm leaving. That's when he punched me in the face and threw my clothes in the hall, saying, you shitty fag, get lost or I'll hit you again.

The fact was that Maria and I weren't having any luck with our adventures.

We continued with the same routine, movies, dinners, parties, and a lot of work. Every Saturday we played golf. One morning I couldn't go. Maria went alone and accepted an invitation to play a game with a German guy. His name was Klaus and he was in the country for a two-week visit. Afterward they had lunch by the pool. That's what she told me, and that evening she invited him to have dinner with her.

As always, I helped Maria get ready. I didn't let her put on the red dress we'd bought because it had brought her bad luck. Maria laughed, saying she didn't believe my absurd superstitions (her words), but even so she didn't wear it.

I didn't see her come home and the first thing I did in the morning was make her breakfast, put it on a tray, and take it to her room. I wanted to hear all about it. She smiled happily, talking about the German. She said Klaus was friendly, intelligent, charming, he had a great sense of humor, he wasn't good-looking but he was very interesting.

Unlike me, Maria liked ugly men. I think that's the only thing we disagreed about. Maria decided she would take him to see Paratí. I asked if they had made love and she answered with a shy laugh, not yet, we're not in a hurry. But he is a good kisser.

I packed Maria's bag. She and Klaus left for Paratí on a Friday, and they would return two days later.

Sunday night Maria didn't show up. She didn't come back on Monday. On Tuesday she left a message on the answering machine saying she was fine, not to worry. On Wednesday I couldn't sleep. On Thursday I had to take a very strong dose of sleeping pills to sleep just three hours. The same thing happened every day until Maria finally came back. The entire week she had spent in Parati, she only called once. I didn't tell her that it had hurt me because I didn't want to get in the way of her happiness. Maria was obviously in love.

As soon as she got home she embraced me, and as she kissed me, she said, Joãozinho, my love, I have to talk to you. She kissed me more and laughingly told me what I least wanted to hear: I'm crazy in love. I'm going away with Klaus. We're going to get married and live in Berlin. I even know the address: Schlutterstrasse 12. She repeated the address emphasizing every syllable, she could even pronounce the number twelve in German. I think that Maria noticed, from my silence, that I was sad, and she embraced me again, asking, aren't you happy for me? The only thing I could manage to say was, you should be happy. Now I'm going to run over to the drugstore to get a prescription.

I walked along the street. I went into a drugstore to buy a bottle of aspirin to buy time and justify my artful pretext. To be truthful I didn't want Maria to notice how sad I was. Going back home I thought, I don't have the right to pressure her and make a show of my suffering; if I love her, as in fact I do, I should be happy for her that she is happy. I wiped my face with my hands.

I helped Maria in every way I could to prepare for her trip. I did everything possible to hide my depression. I took her to the airport.

In the taxi, on the way home, I looked out the window at the landscape. It was night.

For the first time in my life I got thin as a skeleton. I stopped eating, bathing, I spent my days prostrate in bed, in a state of complete apathy.

I heard the doorbell ring. I wasn't interested. They insisted. Even so, I stayed in the bed, with my eyes closed.

Life at Risk

I was unhappy and knew why. I'm not one of those people who go looking for problems and suffer for no reason.

I spent the night at Cláudio's apartment. I didn't sleep well. When he woke up, I had already read the newspaper and made breakfast.

As soon as he went into the bathroom and I heard the sound of the shower, I sneaked back into the bedroom and searched the pockets of Cláudio's pants and coat and his wallet. On his check stubs, only expenses connected with his car and dinners with me. I looked for his cell phone. Didn't find it. The briefcase he used at work had a combination and was locked. I memorized the six numbers, three on one clasp and three on the other, that were showing. I tried various combinations of numbers, without success. I couldn't get it open. I put back the original numbers so he wouldn't suspect I had been going through his things.

I returned to the living room to wait for him. I was sitting on the sofa, pretending to read the newspaper, when I heard his cell phone ring in the other room. I was certain that Cláudio had answered. Silently, I went back to the bedroom door, which was closed. He was speaking softly, and I couldn't understand what he was saying. Abruptly, I turned the doorknob. When he saw me he hastily turned off the phone.

"Hurry up, love," I said to cover up, "breakfast's going to get cold."

It wasn't the first time that had happened. Cláudio had been distant and moody. He didn't answer his cell phone in front of me, and whenever I'd spend the night at his place he turned off the sound on the answering machine. I was puzzled. After all, who would be calling him at that early hour?

We said little to each other during breakfast.

"What time are you leaving for work?" he asked.

"In an hour." I was lying, because the question aroused my suspicions. I decided not to go the office. I would stay at Cláudio's to get to the bottom of things. I detest suspecting people, but my head was filled with suspicion. I'm a woman no different from any other. Maybe they're all like that, jealous and possessive.

I accompanied Cláudio to the hallway and waited till he got into the elevator. I made sure by checking the luminous dial that he had descended to the garage. At the window I spied from behind the curtain until I saw his car leave. Then I called my office to say I'd be coming in late.

Cláudio's place was crammed with books, magazines, old newspapers. An immense amount of paper. Not to mention the fact that he was the type who never threw anything away. I was in doubt as to where to begin. I decided on the living room, because it housed a kind of library where his computer was, along with several cabinets. I opened one of them, then another and another. It was going to take a lot of work, because there was a slew of folders, boxes, envelopes.

I sat on the floor and carefully went through folder after folder. It took an enormous amount of time. I placed them in their respective spots. I found a box full of photographs. Many of them of Cláudio's family and him as a child. Among them was a photo of a suntanned woman in a bikini. Her body was shapely. I supposed Cláudio had had an affair with the girl. On the back, a heart drawn in red with the names Tati and Cláudio. I was right. There was no date, but judging by the look of the paper it was old. I saw other photos. The same short-haired woman in different pictures. In many of them she was nude, in sensual poses. They had been taken in Cláudio's bedroom.

I analyzed the photos carefully. The bedroom was just like it was. The bedspread was the same, the wall was painted the same shade of blue, the same print curtain and carpeted floor. They were recent photographs. I chose the ones in which the woman looked the prettiest and ripped them up. I felt hatred because, no denying it, she was beautiful, much prettier than me. I ended up tearing into tiny bits all the photos of that shameless bitch who let herself be photographed naked.

I opened a drawer and a swarm of slides appeared before me. I held them up to the light; most of them of some museum, which was of no interest. As I looked at each one, I threw it on the floor. Until I saw another nude woman's body: a profile with short hair, a breast, the nape of a neck, a face out of focus. It looked like the same woman. I crushed the slides in my hands. I started pulling out drawers, searching everything. Then I went to the computer desk, looked through all the pieces of paper with written notes. One of them had a telephone number on it. I dialed the number. An answering machine with a woman's voice. I shredded the paper and tossed it into the air as if it were confetti.

I sensed he was cheating on me, but there was only one way to prove it—reading his e-mails.

I couldn't start his computer because it asked for a password. I hit the computer, once, twice, then got a metal ashtray and smashed the monitor, the case, the keyboard. I threw the mouse against the wall. The computer never had a password before. Why did it have one now? It was obvious, I couldn't be more right. He was cheating on me.

I shoved everything on the desk onto the floor. I pulled down the curtains and tried to rip them. I couldn't. I went to the kitchen and got a large knife. I cut them to pieces.

Obeying an impulse, I stabbed the cushions and shredded the stuffing.

That was when Cláudio opened the door without my noticing it. I only became aware of his presence when he said, "What is this? Are you crazy?"

I wasn't scared; I never get scared. I had one arm raised over my head, still holding the knife, and without moving I faced him. "I may be a lot of things, but crazy isn't one of them."

Cláudio paled, and drawing back, said, frightened, "Please, don't hurt me."

I lowered my arm and he, thinking I was going to attack him, ran away. That hadn't even crossed my mind. I heard his rapid steps toward the stairs.

I went back to the bedroom. I took off my nightgown, put on my clothes, and went into the bathroom to comb my hair. I thought, How could I like such a coward? If he loved me, he'd risk being knifed by me.

As I left I saw the ripped curtains, the slides scattered on the floor, the broken computer monitor, all the damage I'd done, and thought, He wasn't worth any of this. I should have kicked his ass out long ago.

Waiting

There was a time when Alberto slept very well, close to eight hours a night in a deep sleep. But that didn't happen anymore, and as night approached he would become uneasy. He tried to read, watch television, but nothing relaxed him enough to sleep.

Ever since he had retired from his professorship at the university, he took his breakfast daily at the corner bakery. One day, while eating toast with coffee and orange juice, he felt his death must be near.

When he got home, he opened the newspaper to the obituary section. VITOR DUARTE SAMPAIO was the heading in bold face. Maria Lúcia. Marisa, Jayme, and family announce his passing. Interment will take place today at eleven o'clock, at the Order of Carmo Cemetery.

Alberto read all the other funeral announcements and noticed that five of the seven deceased were men. He rose to get a pen and his cell phone. He sat down again beside the newspaper. Then he underlined those who were male. He dialed Information and asked for the phone numbers of those men. Only one of the deceased was unlisted.

He called and gave a fictitious name, claiming to work for a research center. He asked for information about the age of the deceased, the cause, the time of death, and whether by any chance they had uttered any last words, like Goethe, who said, "More light!" Alberto jotted down the data that he'd gathered. Vitor Duarte Sampaio, seventy-two: heart attack. João Ribeiro, seventy-four: lung cancer. Nelson Brito Costa, ninety-three: a fall at home, died instantly. Mauricio Alencar, fifty-one: unknown causes.

Of all these, only Mauricio Alencar had uttered any last words when he died: "What the shit is this disease that's killing me?"

The information made Alberto nervous. He thought, I don't want to die without knowing the cause. Of course, there were also unexpected ends like accidents and other such things.

The next day, Alberto checked into the hospital and had a complete check-up done to make sure he was one hundred percent healthy.

He decided to visit his mother, Arlete, on a Friday, because that was the day she invited seven female friends over to play cards. This would allow him to leave after fifteen minutes. His mother, by herself, prepared an enormous number of hors d'oeuvres to serve her friends. Zefa, the maid, helped mainly by washing the dishes and pans.

Arlete always applied makeup and wore a different wig. She had a closet full of wigs of various cuts and colors. Alberto didn't take part in the game; he hated playing cards, besides never being invited.

"Son," said Arlete, who was ninety-four, "if I die, I'd like you to buy a house for Zefa, after all, she's worked here for many years." Alberto found it strange that his mother had said *if I die*. He thought, does Mom think she's not going to die? She should have said, *when I die*, buy a house for Zefa. He kissed his mother good-bye and said, "Rest assured: I'll buy Zefa a house."

The week went by slowly, with Alberto anxiously awaiting the test results. Every morning he read the obituaries in the newspaper. Using the same methods, he called the dead person's home and obtained the information he wanted. Again, only one of the dead had said something, by coincidence a professor with whom he was acquainted, Pedro Monteiro, also retired. Monteiro had said: "I am in flames!" It was the professor's wife herself who supplied this information, adding that her husband was delirious, because the air conditioning was on. Alberto thought, This ignoramus doesn't know it's the phrase David Hume uttered as he died. "I am in flames!" was a phrase that had always bothered Alberto because, like him, Hume was an atheist. He felt a shiver, as if death were present.

When night came, Alberto would lie down and turn

on the television. He recalled his notes, in which he'd recorded that the majority of the dead had passed away at night. Alberto only managed to get to sleep at daybreak. Afterward, when he woke up, he wouldn't even have breakfast at the bakery but walked down the street unable to control the emotions that ran through his head, leaving him more and more anxious.

One day he concluded that the majority of the deceased were buried. Death liked cemeteries, flowers, coffins, priests, sermons, prayers, mourners. He called a cab and in a matter of minutes was at a notary's office. He had a document drawn up that stated he wished to be cremated and have his ashes planted at the root of a royal palm like those in the Botanical Garden. Surely death would be less interested in cremated people.

He stopped at a lunch stand to eat. When he got home, Carminha handed him the envelope from the hospital. Alberto read the tests of blood, feces, and urine, looked at the x-rays and CAT scan of his head. The reports said his heath was good. That doesn't mean a thing, thought Alberto, death comes when you least expect it. That same day, a Friday, Zefa called to say that Alberto's mother had choked on her food and died.

He dashed to his mother's apartment. He was received by Zefa and the seven old women in tears. Arlete was still sitting at the table, her head resting on the deck of cards. First, he called an ambulance, and the doctor confirmed his mother's death. Then he contacted a mortuary for removal of the body and subsequent burial. He also wrote the funeral notice—actually copied from the first one he came across in the paper. ARLETE CUNHA in boldface type. Alberto Cunha announces the passing of his beloved mother and issues an invitation for the interment, which will take place today, at ten o'clock, at São João Batista Cemetery.

At the funeral, Alberto told Zefa that he would sell his mother's apartment and buy her a house in the district where Zefa lived. The maid didn't like Alberto but was so moved that she kissed his hand.

After the seventh-day mass, he thought: I'm next. But nothing happened. After the thirtieth-day mass, he went home convinced that this time he wouldn't escape. He stayed at home waiting for death to seek him out. But it didn't come and didn't come. He turned on the television.

I'm going to wait for death watching television, he thought, as he ate cookies.

A Trivial Story

Vivi analyzed her face with a magnifying mirror in the bathroom. She turned on all the lights and began slowly turning her head. She carefully observed every detail, whether there was a hair still to be removed from her upper lip, eyebrows, and chin, some blackhead to be squeezed. Then she washed her face with a special liquid soap and, using a rough sponge, made light circular motions in order not to irritate the skin. She applied a toning lotion to close the pores and ended her ritual with anti-wrinkle cream, sunblock 60, and makeup.

She was seventeen years old and very worried because she had noticed wrinkles around her mouth and eyes. The only reason she didn't quit smoking was fear of putting on weight. She weighed herself three times a day, when she got up, in mid-afternoon, and before going to bed. Each time, she measured her percentage of body fat with an instrument. She claimed one couldn't rely on just a scale. She had already done liposuction, at the age of fifteen, on her abdomen and upper thighs. It had been a birthday present from her parents, after much insistence. They never failed to grant her every wish.

Before going to bed she would take a box of laxatives, but her body was accustomed to that type of medication and she therefore needed to ingest a large quantity of pills to be able to go to the bathroom. She loved having diarrhea. She would sit on the toilet and leaf through fashion magazines. She would clip one or another page to get ideas on how she should dress.

She also watched television, which she tried to avoid because she always ended up compulsively stuffing herself with junk food while watching those stupid programs. Later she would regret it and have to force herself to vomit. She found that unpleasant.

She hated her father and mother because she considered them idiots. Vivi lived in a beautiful apartment, had a house in the mountains, traveled abroad every year, but everything was shit. It irritated her that her credit card had a limit.

She would go up and down escalators, and killed herself to conform to the patterns of beauty. Happiness constantly lay in the next purchase. She went out every night, cut her classes, and now and then would faint in the street from not eating. She found nothing enjoyable. She would dance entire nights in the company of people she disdained, downing Ecstasy with a bottle of mineral water in her hand. Her boyfriend worked in television and appeared in celebrity magazines, which she also disdained because she considered them poor and tacky, a band of nobodies low-born, exhibitionist and opportunistic, all of them damned imbeciles. Women became famous for their asses and breasts. To Vivi, only the rabble had asses and breasts. She told the actor to go to hell, he was a fifth-rater from the outskirts.

She was in the habit of thinking: What people! What a culture! This country is a lost cause! They're all amoral. The have-nots do everything to get money, power, or just to become famous. And the haves think they've got the right to demand anything they want. Vivi came to the conclusion that money could buy anything.

She was also aggressive with her wealthy friends, dim-wits, daddy's boys. She suffered from being surrounded by a bunch of slackers. She hated that mediocre society of total cretins. But she also did everything she could to belong to it.

She was bored. She felt a kind of unbearable distress that made her view people, things, and facts with repugnance. Frequently, Vivi would observe her mother's dog, a gray miniature schnauzer, always lying calmly. She wasn't aware of it, but as she concentrated on the animal, something that wasn't herself, her boredom decreased. At times she wished she could be a dog or a cat, in order not to feel the anguish of living that seemed to her the origin of everything bad.

She began snorting cocaine to pass the time. She lost weight and was happy to see her skinny reflection in the mirror. She loved feeling the arrhythmic beating of her heart. She maxed out her credit cards with cash advances, called a friend who had a dealer, and went out to buy coke. She snorted. Bought more blow. Snorted. More blow.

One day, when she got home she found her father and mother waiting for her, ready for a serious conversation. They were frightened by Vivi's appearance, spoke of their concern. Her parents started arguing and forgot their daughter. They all had dinner together, in silence.

Vivi snorted more coke, breathing deeply in hopes of recreating the experience of the first time. Nothing. She would snort several times a day. The euphoria, the excitation, and the illusory surge of energy weren't the same; after half an hour the depression returned even stronger, which led her to consume another dose to revive her morbid well-being, then another dose, more depression, another dose, followed by yet more depression.

Her suffering, her unhappiness became even greater. Nothing succeeded in ending the daily boredom of living. She became even more disturbed. Yes, Vivi knew that everyone feels bored, that there's no one who doesn't, but some people manage to pretend they don't suffer from it. But there it was, in the depths of her being, tormenting her. They say it's easy to be happy just by wanting to. And if you're happy, maybe the boredom won't be as bad. And if Vivi told herself, "I'm happy," would she believe it?

She started injecting the drug. She slept less and less.

She stopped getting an allowance, her credit cards were canceled. She sold her jewels. Like all addicts, she began stealing money from her parents, along with household utensils, to buy drugs.

She took a taxi to the favela. She snorted, brightness, darkness, injected, brightness, darkness, darkness, snorted, brightness and darkness and darkness and brightness, brightness, darkness . . . It was a succession of metamorphoses . . .

After wandering around the spots where the drug was sold, she met Uóston, who was fascinated by the white chick from down below. Uóston was the kingpin of the drug trade, and finding this out excited Vivi. Free coke was quite a turn-on. To her, this was a real man. One who did what he wanted, who was a menace to society, who lived by his own laws.

They went to his shack, they fucked and snorted coke. She spent the night there. When she woke up, she was alone. But, before she could conclude that the place was a hovel, Uóston showed up with blow.

She spent the day restlessly pacing up and down, waiting for Uóston to return with the drug. She looked at the dirty, lopsided walls of the shack, which smelled bad, a mixture of sewage, damp, and the smell of grease coming from the neighboring house. Nauseated, she tried to vomit but couldn't. She ransacked everything, looking for a speck of cocaine. Nothing. She looked for money. She was becoming more and more agitated, sweating. Her hair was plastered against her neck.

Uóston came in. Vivi pushed him away when he said he hadn't brought any powder. She screamed and broke everything in reach. Uóston grabbed her by the hair and threw her out the door. She fell to the ground and he kicked her.

Vivi went to another favela. She offered her body in exchange for blow. Skinnier by the day, weak, suffering mood swings, delusions of persecution.

She wandered and danced entire nights, shaking her body, going from hand to hand, bending down, kneeling, spreading her legs. She was indifferent to what she did. She knew what she wanted. The urgency to satisfy her desire grew greater and greater. Boredom had abandoned her, for boredom is an attribute of the sane. The future no longer existed. She was alone with her hallucinations and a constant nausea that more and more tormented her. She would vomit, sick to her stomach. Boom, boom, boom, boom, boom, boom, the music played even louder in her head. She thought her ears would explode. She could no longer stay on her feet. She fell. Something warm ran down her legs. Crawling, she dragged herself to the exit of the place where she was. Even in the silence of the street her head throbbed.

Boom, boom, boom, boom, boom, boom, she pressed her hands against her ears. The sun had come up. Where was she? She didn't know. She writhed from the pain in her belly. Vivi didn't realize it, but the urine went on running down her legs. She trembled from pain, panic. She screamed, "What is this place?" The music went on hammering in her head. "What is this place? Where am I?" A woman passing by in the street explained where she was. It didn't make sense. Vivi looked at the woman, perplexed. The woman got onto a bus with Vivi and left her at a public hospital.

Vivi wasn't able to fill out a form, but even so she waited in line. After a long wait she was directed to the infectious disease ward. They gave her some injections and took blood for tests. She was kept overnight in the hospital. The next morning, a doctor handed her an envelope. "You're pregnant," he said. She got up and went to the infirmary bathroom. She pulled her hair back and looked at herself in the mirror. How long since she had done that, look at herself in the mirror.

She left the hospital and sat on a bench on the sidewalk. She didn't see the people, the buses, the cars passing in front of her. All she felt was the sun warming her skin.

Home, Sweet Home

My only chance, and I missed it. Do I regret it? I don't know.

The hairdresser was waiting for me. Today I'm going to lighten my hair, I said. You finally decided. The hairdresser moved away. I called Jorge, my husband. When she comes back, I said, I'm just getting a blow-dry. I asked her to hurry, because I had to get home before six. I left in a rush.

The first thing I did when I got home was kiss my two daughters and see what they had for homework. When they heard their father arrive, they ran to greet him, and I followed them. "I want a kiss from my three little girls." The three of us hugged him. A short time later Jorge told me to get dressed for dinner at Álvaro Pimentel's house. When my husband came into the bedroom, I was ready. He looked at me and said delicately, "What's with that dress? It's too low-cut. Why the red lipstick? It doesn't look good on you. Please remove that lipstick and put on that black dress I like." I tried to argue with Jorge, saying I'd bought the dress the day before, especially for the Pimentel dinner. "Rita, dear," he interrupted, "tomorrow you can exchange it for something else. That neckline is very inappropriate, I'd even say vulgar. I don't like for my wife to go around like that." I put on the dress that Jorge requested, I didn't feel good, I looked at myself, dissatisfied, saw the red lipstick and removed it before he could say anything else. Jorge came out of the bathroom wrapped in a towel and praised me. "Now then, you look beautiful. Sweetheart, while I finish getting ready, see if the girls need any help with their homework." I spent half an hour with them until he called me to leave for the dinner at Pimentel's house.

There were lots of people invited. We greeted the host. Jorge joined the men and I sat down beside Marlene, my best friend, sipping champagne. After dinner, Jorge came up and said, "Rita, let me have my cigar, please." I looked for it in my purse. Bad luck, I'd forgotten it. I apologized. "Sweetheart," Jorge said, "don't you care anymore about the things I ask?" I apologized again. Jorge left and, ill at ease, I looked at Marlene, who had witnessed the scene. Marlene called the waiter and got two glasses of champagne. I downed mine in a single swallow. Alcohol always left me feeling euphoric. I was still drinking when Jorge approached and said, "We're leaving." I placed the glass of champagne on a nearby table, gave Marlene a kiss on the cheek, and left, leaning on my husband's arm.

Twice a week I had pottery classes—I made plates, pots, vases, that sort of thing. I always left before the class was over, but that day I had to wait for a vase to come out of the kiln and was late. When I got home, the first thing I saw was Jorge standing in the living room. I asked about the children. "First I want to talk to you," he said. "You know how I detest coming home and not finding you waiting for me, don't you?" I tried to explain that I was at pottery class and he interrupted, saying, "Dear, the reason doesn't matter; I just hope it won't happen again. Shall we have dinner?"

The next day I invited Marlene for lunch. Over dessert she asked if I sometimes wished my husband would die. Of course not, I replied. "But every married woman feels that way at some time," Marlene insisted, "especially if he's rich like yours. No wife wants a poor husband to die—who'd pay for the children's milk?" I asked Marlene if she wanted her husband to die. "I do," she said, "and the only reason I don't kill him at times like that is because I need him to buy milk for the children."

At that moment the maid served dessert, a chocolate mousse. "I made the mousse myself, you have to try it, Marlene." My friend tried it and said it was delicious. "It's easy to make," I explained, "eggs, semisweet chocolate, sugar, and whipping cream. Then all you do is mix it well and put it in the refrigerator. When it's for Jorge, I also add *liqueur de cacao*, because that's the way he likes it."

"Do you do everything the way your husband likes it?"

asked Marlene. I changed the subject and asked if she'd like some coffee. "You didn't answer my question," said Marlene.

"Or you mine. Do you want some coffee or not?"

On Sunday I woke up early. As usual, I tiptoed in order not to wake Jorge. I went to the children's room, spoke to the nanny, the children were making a lot of noise. I went to the kitchen, got a couple of cookies from a tin, chewed them quickly so that Jorge wouldn't appear out of nowhere and catch me eating. I asked the cook how preparations for the *feijoada* were coming along. Jorge's sister, her husband, and two teenage sons were having lunch with us. My daughters came running into the kitchen with the nanny. "Mommy, can we go play at Carol's house?" I said yes. I grabbed two more cookies from the tin, served myself some black coffee. At that moment I heard Jorge's voice calling me from the living room. He had woken up. I set the cup on the sink, ran my tongue over my teeth to make sure they were clean, and ran out of the kitchen.

"Rita, you didn't have your coffee without me, did you?"

"Of course not," I replied, "you know I always wait for you." We sat down at the table. The cook brought the coffee.

"Let's eat lunch in the garden," he said, "we can have a barbecue."

I explained that I'd already begun preparing the *fei-joada* that he'd requested. Jorge interrupted me, saying he preferred barbecue. Then he wanted to know where the girls were. When I told him they were off playing at a friend's house, he criticized me for letting them leave without his permission. I justified myself by pointing out that he'd been sleeping. But Jorge refused to hear it, saying I should have waited for him to wake up so he could authorize their going. Then he went to take a bath and said he wanted the girls back home immediately. All these remarks were delicately made.

On Sundays he always took a leisurely bath in the tub doing crosswords. I called the cook and told her that lunch would be barbecue. From the kitchen I called the nanny and said that Mr. Jorge wanted the girls back home. I didn't succeed in reading the newspaper. I helped the cook prepare lunch. The children arrived, unhappy, avoiding my hugs. I felt like crying. I left the kitchen and went into the bedroom.

Jorge was still in the tub, no doubt concentrating on his crossword puzzle. I noticed the smell of gas. I knocked softly on the door. No answer. I turned the knob and from the doorway saw Jorge, his mouth open, his face white, stretched out in the tub, his head hanging to one side, the crosswords magazine floating in the water. He had fainted. I contemplated his body for some time. I didn't turn off the gas. I closed the bathroom door. Left the bedroom. Walked slowly to the living room. I heard the voices of the children playing. I sat down in an armchair, tense.

I closed my eyes. Waiting, waiting. Until I couldn't take it anymore. I ran back to the bathroom. With difficulty, I took Jorge's body out of the tub and dragged him to the hallway. I kneeled on the floor beside the body, gave him mouth-to-mouth resuscitation, massaged and hit his chest. Jorge came to. He stared at me as he regained his breath. Then he said, haltingly, "Rita . . . didn't I ask you . . . to have that water heater . . . checked? Go get my robe."

That was my only chance, and I missed it. Do I regret it? I don't know.

The Lady of Solitude

Inspector Barcelos rang the doorbell. A tall woman with red hair and blue eyes ringed with black answered the door. He asked, "Are you the Dona Clarisse who phoned the precinct saying there was a person dead from a gunshot here in your house?"

She stared at the inspector, took a drag on her cigarette and, letting out the smoke, replied that she was. Then she gestured for him to follow her.

They went into a bedroom. A man with a head wound was sitting in an armchair. From a superficial examination, Inspector Barcelos saw that the victim had been dead for some time. He asked how it had happened, and Clarisse replied that it had been during the night before. Barcelos took out his cell phone and called the precinct to request a forensics team. Then he asked Clarisse to tell him how it all had happened.

She handed him a sheet of paper, saying that everything was explained there, as she'd spent the night writing. The inspector asked her to tell the story aloud, but she refused, saying that she was in no condition to do so.

While he waited for the forensics team, Inspector Barcelos read:

I have always lived alone, accompanied by my books and my solitude. Everything I know about myself, about others, about the world, especially about myself, I learned from poets, my dear friends who have never abandoned me. I take them with me wherever I go, whether alone or accompanied. One poet once told me that I, in this moment of disjunction, "lost myself inside of me because I was a labyrinth and today, when I feel anything, it is longing for myself."

I am writing this letter lying on the floor beside the body of R. I didn't want him to be alone.

In my profession it is inadvisable to become too enthusiastic about someone of flesh and blood. We have to control the situation to protect ourselves. That's why I have my secrets. I write my mysteries in the air. In the silences of the spoken, as another poet said, "the silence, upon silence, usurps from silence its meager work."

What was the first time like? R. looked at me at length, as if discovering me with his gaze. I was naked in bed. It was our first encounter. He wanted to know my real name. Clarisse, I answered. He extended his hand, ran it softly over my face. I closed my eyes. I felt the touch of his tongue as if he were probing the taste of my skin. He breathed in the scent of my body in all its contours. I opened my eyes. By the expression on his face I realized he wanted to explore me through his five senses. We made love and afterward lay side by side. I rested my head on R.'s chest, and he embraced me and caressed my hair.

Inspector Barcelos stopped reading and said there was nothing there about the facts he was investigating. Clarisse asked him to read to the end. Sighing, the inspector resumed reading.

I'm a prostitute. There's something romantic and seductive in that profession, even more so when, like me, you can choose your client. I was happy, like the courtesans in ancient times, beautiful women, independent, often influential, who dressed elegantly, had dignity, and paid their taxes. When they call us dissolute they commit a great insult. A dissolute person is depraved, licentious. Our profession demands discipline and dedication, it's an art. We're artists of pleasure and entertainment.

R. was alerted by Norma, my agent, that before accepting him as a client I would have to interview him. But I liked him as soon as he came into my living room. We went into the bedroom and I asked if he liked poetry, because I always read poems to my clients before making love. I began reading R. a sonnet by Bocage that says: "Fuck each other, ye married and single." R. put his hand over the book and recited the rest of the stanza: "And do so now: for the age is short, and the hours of pleasure fly swiftly away."

I was surprised, not only because he knew the poem by heart but, judging by his way of saying it, he knew it better than I.

I know how to read. And the timing, the rhythm are mine. I make them, and they're not the same as the poet's. I create the emphasis according to my interlocutor, whom I look in the eye the entire time. But R. did it better than I did, and the poem ceased to be mine. I would come to love it or hate it. I surrendered myself to him.

The inspector stopped reading again, saying that what she had written made no sense and asking her to state what had happened. Clarisse said she was going to get him some coffee and left the bedroom. The uniformed policeman in the living room followed her. Barcelos, cursing between his teeth, resumed reading.

I was hopelessly in love. I wrote those words, hopelessly in love, in the air, with the tip of my senses.

I decided to tell that to R., who would be pleased to

move in with me. I added that I wanted to spend the rest of my life at his side. R. laughed and said, Live here? With you? You must be joking. I'm serious, I said, I want to marry you and make you happy. Then R. said sarcastically, You really think I'd marry a whore?

It wasn't the words that hurt me and led me to commit this extreme act. It was the expression of disdain that I saw on his face.

I got the gun I keep in the drawer of the night table and pointed it at him. R. laughed, got up, and said ironically, Go on, give me the weapon. I fired. He fell on the floor. That's all.

Clarisse returned with the coffee. Inspector Barcelos had finished reading. He drank the coffee pensively, then said the text alleged that the victim had fallen to the floor, but now he was sitting in the chair. Furthermore, everything indicated that the victim should be nude. Clarisse explained that she had felt sorry for R. lying on the floor and had decided to dress him and position him in as dignified a pose as possible, sitting in the armchair.

The forensics team arrived. Inspector Barcelos asked Clarisse to go with him to the precinct to make a statement.

As they were leaving, Clarisse asked the inspector to wait

a minute. She went to the bookcase and took down a book, telling Barcelos it was by a poet who understood what was going on. She opened the book and began to recite.

Barcelos led Clarisse by the arm. She continued declaiming the poem.

Paula Parisot was born in Rio de Janeiro. She has a degree in industrial design from the Pontificia Universidade Catolica (Rio de Janeiro) and an M.F.A. from the New School in New York. *The Lady of Solitude*, her first book, was a finalist for the Jabuti Prize for the short story. Her first novel, *Hinges and Screws* (2010), inspired a performance art piece in which the author spent seven days and six nights in a cage, built in imitation of the sanatorium room described in the final scene of the novel. Her most recent book, *Leaving* (2013), is illustrated by the author and has also inspired several performance art and film pieces. The author lives in São Paulo with her family.

Elizabeth Lowe is the founding director of the Center for Translation Studies at the University of Illinois at Urbana-Champaign. She has translated Brazilian and Lusophone writers, including Clarice Lispector, Euclides da Cunha, Machado de Assis, J.P. Cuenca, Antônio Lobo Antunes, and João de Melo. Her translation of J.P. Cuenca's *The Happiest Ending for a Love Story is an Accident* (2013) was a finalist for the IMPAC award. She lives in Gainesville, Florida.

CLIFFORD E. LANDERS is a professor emeritus at New Jersey City University. He has translated more than thirty book-length works from Portuguese, including novels by Rubem Fonseca, João Ubaldo Ribeiro, Jorge Amado, Patrícia Melo, Nélida Piñon, and José de Alencar. A former Fulbright exchange professor in the Dominican Republic, he is a recipient of the Mario Ferreira award and the author of *Literary Translation: A Practical Guide*. He lives with his wife Vasda Bonafini Landers in Naples, Florida.